Death at the Sun Club

Club

A Clara Fitzgerald Mystery

Evelyn James

Red Raven Publications 2024

www.sophie-jackson.com

Chapter One

C lara contemplated the paperwork before her. It consisted of a number of bills that she was plucking up the courage to deposit in a drawer and forget about for a while longer. Clara's recent work had involved clients who could not afford her services at her usual prices but who still desperately needed her assistance. As a result, she was slightly financially embarrassed. It was only a temporary misfortune, for very soon she would be issuing reminders to certain other clients who ought to have paid up, but who had not. People she knew could afford her services, but who were being tardy about settling up their own bills.

Such were the perils of being self-employed, she told herself, and also of being a woman in business. A few too many of her clients supposed they could eke out the time before they had to pay her because she would not hound them like a man would. They assumed she would back down if they tried to avoid paying. They were rapidly disabused of this idea. Clara did not back down, especially when money was involved.

It was just another of those inconveniences about her life that used up far more time than they should.

She was sitting in her office, the one she rented above a

haberdashery shop, taking some time to herself. While she did a lot of her work from her house, it was nice to come to the office where she could be completely alone to work in silence without the distraction of hearing Annie nagging Tommy about leaving his shirts in a heap on the bedroom floor, or her constant interruptions to see if Clara wanted more tea.

Annie meant well, but her constant attention could be somewhat overwhelming. Tommy did not assist either; his own opinions on the paperwork were complicated. While he would sit down and go through bills when duty called, he had a tendency to get overly irate when he realised people hadn't paid. He would threaten to march up to doors and bang on them to demand money, and Clara felt that there were more diplomatic ways to resolve the problem. She did not want the rumour to get around that Clara Fitzgerald had a tendency to send out heavies when she wasn't paid. It might put people off seeking her help. On the other hand, she wanted it to be made clear that she did not stand for people not paying up what they owed her.

The result was that she liked to manage her finances herself, and for the most part, she did so effectively and efficiently. This month was just one of those occasions when certain circumstances had conspired against her.

She had almost reached the point where she had convinced herself to shove the bills into a drawer and forget about them until the next day, when she heard a quiet knock on her office door. The knock had been on her upstairs door; the one on street level was left open so that clients could pop in and wander up to see her. In general, she found most people were slightly intimidated coming up unannounced, and usually sent letters or a message of some description first. But occasionally people did pop in to see her out of the blue.

"Come in," Clara called out.

The door opened briskly, and in walked Mrs Wilton. Clara was never sure whether to smile or sigh when she recognised Mrs Wilton's face. She had been Clara's first ever client and the cases she brought Clara were always interesting, though very often complicated by the woman's personal problems. It was also far too often the case that Mrs Wilton brought cases to Clara on the behalf of people who had not asked for her assistance and who would suddenly be put out to discover that a private detective was prying into their private affairs. Despite being told on more than one occasion by a friend or acquaintance that they did not want Mrs Wilton hiring an investigator just because someone's garden gnomes went missing, or a cat had not been seen for a few days, Mrs Wilton continued on this path. Considering it her civic duty to resolve the small, mundane mysteries of everyday living through Clara.

"Good morning, Mrs Wilton."

"Good morning, Clara," Mrs Wilton nodded at her. "I have come to you on a matter of great urgency. It is a grave business, Clara. Grave indeed."

"Should I put the kettle on then?" Clara asked with a slight smile on her lips.

"I could quite do with a cup to get me over the shock," Mrs Wilton did look somewhat paler than normal.

She settled herself down in the chair before Clara's desk, while Clara rose to start boiling the kettle over the fireplace. She did not have a stove in her office, but the fireplace served the same purpose, even if it was slightly old fashioned to use a hearth for boiling your kettle.

"What is this all about then, Mrs Wilton?" Clara asked.

Mrs Wilton was fussing with her hat, which she was unpinning with great care, laying the long hat pins on Clara's desk before she removed it. Then she put down her handbag.

"I had to take that off. My head felt like it was boiling," she said, patting the top of her head to demonstrate this unexpected heat. "Have you noticed how many young ladies go about all the time with no hat at all? Some men too, it seems quite undignified."

"I tend not to think about it," Clara remarked.

She was bareheaded at that moment in time. Clara had long tawny brown hair which had a natural curl to it. She kept it roughly below her shoulder length and usually in a loose braid. She had not gone in for the latest fashion of having a shingle in her hair and cutting everything in a short bob.

She liked her hair just as it was.

"I dare say one gets used to these things," Mrs Wilton replied. "Honestly, I think that could be what is wrong with this world. Things are all going downhill. This tendency towards uncovering oneself. It starts with the lack of a hat. Then ankles suddenly appear, and before you know it, it's wrists everywhere followed by the lower arms. Why, before we are done who knows how much skin we will all be showing as we walk down the street?"

"I had never given it much thought," Clara remarked, wondering where this was going. "Has someone had their hat stolen?"

"If only the matter was as simple as that," Mrs Wilton groaned. "We are dealing with the moral corruption of the young, Clara. I bring you this matter in great urgency and in great distress. I honestly do not know what will happen if we do not make a stand right here and right now."

"You have my attention, Mrs Wilton. But as yet you have not explained to me exactly what you are talking about. What could be so grave as to cause you this amount of distress?"

Knowing Mrs Wilton as Clara did, it was probably something that anybody else would consider quite mundane. Such as the time when she deemed the lack of potatoes at the grocer's shop a sinister ploy to get people to eat something foreign, like rice, instead.

"I know everyone thinks that I go on about nonsense," Mrs Wilton spoke. "Truthfully, I've had a few people say that directly to my face. I do not take it to heart, however, because, as with all things, the pioneers in this world are usually the ones who are greeted with the most disdain. However, in this instance, I must say that I am not alone among my neighbours in being deeply concerned."

Clara wondered what could have united Mrs Wilton's neighbourhood behind her. She supposed it to be something relatively serious, as most of Mrs Wilton's neighbours tried extremely hard to avoid spending time with the woman. It was not that she was unpleasant company, it was just that once she believed she had a friendship with you, you could expect to see her every day, all day; popping in, delivering small presents, asking you around for dinner. Your life would not be your own anymore. The only reason Clara avoided this sort of relationship with her was because her work meant that she was rarely around to accept the many invitations Mrs Wilton extended to her.

"Now you have convinced me that this is a serious matter," Clara said, thinking that she really needed to move this conversation along so she could get back to doing some actual work. "Why don't you tell me what exactly has caused you such concern?"

Knowing Mrs Wilton, they would spend half an hour while she discussed how the matter she had brought before Clara was going to end the world and change her life forever before they actually got to the root of the matter. Clara suspected it was all part of a ploy to spend as much time in the office as possible. Deep down, Mrs Wilton was actually a very lonely person who struggled to enjoy her own company and needed the constant reassurance of other people around her.

"I am sorry to say this involves my son, Edward," Mrs Wilton said, finally getting around to the matter at hand. "These last couple of years, Edward has not known what to do with himself. He got himself a good job working as an accountant. It suited him immensely. But he found it very boring. He's been drifting around looking for something to keep him amused ever since. While I have managed to convince him to keep his job up, I haven't been able to stop him from trying out various hobbies that he thought might fill the void that he's feeling in his life since the war. He joined a boating club for a while, which alarmed me immensely as I was concerned he might drown. He can't swim, you know. But then it turned out they were using the boating pond, which isn't very deep. So, I was less concerned, but apparently Edward found that tedious after a while. He termed it unmanly. Then he joined a walking club. He went all over the countryside on these hikes along public footpaths. He used to get quite rattled when he found out a farmer was blocking a right of way. There were a couple of unpleasant moments when he confronted such landowners. That at least got him through the summer, but I sensed that he was starting to grow tired of that too.

"One day he came home with a strange look in his eye and a secretiveness about him. He no longer wanted to talk about the walking club, and I sensed that he had found some other hobby to attract him, something he preferred I did not know about. I racked my brain for possibilities. Perhaps, I thought, he has taken up at last with that winemaking club that I had insisted he keep away from since I felt it was immoral. How was I to know that what he would pick instead would be even worse?"

Despite herself, Clara was intrigued. She leaned her elbows on the desk.

"What hobby has he taken up?" She asked, wondering what could have alarmed Mrs Wilton more than winemaking.

Mrs Wilton's eyes widened, and there was a slight tremor in her voice as she spoke.

"My dear Clara, it is horrific. My darling Edward has joined a nudist club!"

Chapter Two

C lara did not immediately react to Mrs Wilton's stark statement. That was partly because she was not entirely sure what a nudist club was. She did not like to admit her ignorance, but at the same time she was feeling slightly baffled by the statement and was not sure how to go about eliciting the information from Mrs Wilton without appearing to be ignorant.

Mrs Wilton saved her the problem.

"It is called the Brighton Sun Club. Edward says it is the first in the country of its kind, but the idea has been going around for a while. The whole point is to go to this place and... and..." Mrs Wilton had to catch her breath before she could carry on, "one takes off all of one's clothes and wanders around as bare skinned as the day one was born."

Clara found herself for once in her life lost for words. Mrs Wilton, fortunately, could fill the gap sufficiently.

"Edward explains it's something to do with the naturist movement. These people have been around for several years purporting that it is better for the human body to go around unclad and that there is nothing immoral or scandalous about such a thing. They disguise their practises under the banner of the English Gymnosophical Society. Which makes it sound far more proper than it actually is.

People give these things fancy titles to make it seem that there isn't something indecent going on."

"People actually join a club so they can walk around with no clothes on?" Clara had to admit this was quite a radical idea and something that she had never contemplated before.

Like most women of her generation, she had been brought up to always be properly covered in clothing. The human body was not something that anyone should be looking upon unless you happened to be married to the said person, or you were in hospital and requiring treatment, and even then great care would be taken to not expose more of the patient's naked flesh than was absolutely necessary. As a nurse during the war, Clara had been taught to take great pains in maintaining people's dignity by only allowing their naked bodies to be revealed to medical staff, and even then, only the essential bits.

Only children ran around without their clothes on and even then it was only very young children. Very swiftly girls, especially, were raised to wear several layers of clothing. The most recent fad for bathing in relatively skimpy swimsuits had already caused a scandal the last few summers. Sea bathing had been a common activity in Brighton for well over 200 years, but the ladies, and even the gentlemen, were always expected to cover themselves up. Wearing long bathing suits which covered all the majority of the body and using bathing huts which could be wheeled out into the sea so that ladies could enter, change into a bathing suit, and then step out into the waters with a good deal of privacy. After they had taken the waters, they returned to the bathing chamber to exchange their clothes once again. The most prudish of ladies still used these bathing huts, though many younger girls were quite content to wear long one-piece swimsuits and sit out on the beach.

Every summer the old matrons of Brighton would wander along

the promenade staring down at the beach and utter their shock at how much skin the girls were showing. But even this was not excessive. Most ladies' swimsuits covered the knees and stretched right up to the shoulders. Bare arms and lower legs were the only thing that really showed.

Clara recalled there were usually several petitions going around Brighton each summer protesting that the young were walking around indecently clad, and that something ought to be done. But aside from certain restrictions being occasionally attempted, nothing really changed. Supposedly there was a male bathing beach and a female bathing beach, and the two were not supposed to intersect, though truth be told, they quite regularly did. The police rather ignored the matter.

Clara supposed she should not be surprised that someone had taken the next logical step in this transformation of societal expectations. When one had reached the point where only a swimsuit existed between a person's skin and the eyes of a casual viewer, then there was only one way things could go.

"I have never heard of the naturist movement or nudist clubs," Clara said to Mrs Wilton, finally deciding to admit her ignorance. She was not going to be able to bluff her way through the matter.

"I was certainly shocked myself when I heard about it," Mrs Wilton agreed. "Never, in all my days, had I thought I would hear of something so absurd. Well, you suppose such a thing might happen among some of these terribly immoral young people who do things such as take drugs and have debauched parties. But never something that would be acceptable in regular society."

Mrs Wilton had carefully lowered her voice to a whisper when she had spoken about taking drugs, as if just saying it out loud was to condone it.

"Precisely what does one do at a nudist club once one has taken off all their clothes?" Clara said, feeling her way around the subject uneasily.

"Edward says you do anything you want, just like a regular holiday club," Mrs Wilton shrugged. "He talked about playing table tennis and apparently there are swimming pools. Though this particular nudist club has acquired a piece of private beach so that people can take to the waters completely naked. Honestly, Clara, I cannot think what to say. It will corrupt the young, you know?"

"But it *is* private," Clara pointed out. "People can't randomly go there and strip off their clothes?"

"No, my understanding is it is a members only club. And there are strict rules in place, or so Edward tells me. But the whole point is that people are walking around with no clothes on. I don't care what rules they have in place, it's not right."

"I am not sure it's actually illegal either," Clara said. "I mean it could be something to look into. What precisely do you want me to do about it?"

Mrs Wilton looked at Clara aghast, as if she could not suppose that Clara had actually asked such a ridiculous question.

"I expect you to stop him," she said. "In fact, the whole thing ought to be stopped. I have spoken to my neighbours on the subject, and they are all quite agreed. We do not want to live in a town where such things are allowed to happen. The worst of it is the piece of beach they bought is not that far from where I live. I have contemplated it long and hard, and I do believe that if I looked just the right angle through one of my windows at the front, down to the cliffs, I could just see the very edge of that stretch of beach. Supposing one day I wander into my living room, not thinking about anything in particular, glance down, and there is a naked man lying on the sand, and I see... Well, I see everything?"

The horror that accompanied this statement from Mrs Wilton almost amused Clara. She did imagine it would be quite a shock for the poor woman to see a gentleman unclad. While Mrs Wilton had been married and had indulged in the usual benefits of marriage to result in having young Edward, she was of a generation who did such things quietly and discreetly, usually with the lights off.

"It would seem to me this ought to be a matter for the county council. Presumably, they have given permission for this activity to go on?" Clara suggested.

"I spoke to Mr Clayton on the matter," Mrs Wilton agreed. "Do you know him, Clara?"

Clara could safely say she knew very few of the county councillors as she kept as far away from them as possible. Politics had a tendency to raise her temper and she chose to avoid anyone who was heavily involved in them. She had dealt with a few politicians over the course of her cases and, on the whole, she would prefer not to deal with them again.

"No, I cannot say I do know him," she responded to Mrs Wilton.

"Mr Clayton is a personal friend," Mrs Wilton said, somewhat proudly. "I speak to him regularly about things going on in the town and those relating specifically to my neighbourhood. He is always very responsive to my questions and pleased for further information."

Clara wondered if Mr Clayton also considered Mrs Wilton a personal friend, or whether he just aimed to keep as far away from her as possible, and to get rid of her as quickly as he could when she brought a matter to his attention.

"He has informed me that without evidence of illegal activities and improper behaviour, we can do nothing. As long as the club members are abiding by the club rules and not doing anything that could be considered a public nuisance, then all is well because it is private land. They are perfectly entitled to lay there without their clothes on. It's only when you're out in public naked that apparently it is a crime. I call that terrible, Clara. Absolutely terrible."

"I suppose it would be no different to someone being in their back garden with their clothes off," Clara shrugged. "That is private land, after all."

"One cannot go around exposing oneself to the public," Mrs Wilton said firmly. "But apparently it does not classify as exposing oneself when one does it within the confines of a club where such a thing is allowed, and everybody agrees to it."

Mrs Wilton looked quite depressed by this statement.

"Again, Mrs Wilton, I am not sure what you expect from me," Clara said. "Exactly what do you think I can do about this matter?"

"Why, Clara, you can go in and investigate. You can find out that they're doing improper and illegal things and get the evidence we need to shut down the Sun Club."

"Have you any reason to suppose that they're doing these illegal and improper things you mention?"

"Clara, how can you ask such a thing? They are taking their clothes off!"

As in many situations with Mrs Wilton, Clara could see that logical argument was not going to work. She was going to hammer on about the situation until something new distracted her. Clara supposed it would not hurt to investigate and confirm that the Sun Club was following all the rules that they were supposed to be following. Maybe she would have a quiet word with Edward Wilton and suggest that he kept his association with the club very secret from his mother. Maybe he even could tell her that he had given up his membership. That would probably settle her quite quickly, and they could carry on with their lives as long as he kept his activities with the club completely private.

In any case, Clara was not going to get Mrs Wilton out of her office without agreeing to do something, so she did exactly that. She said she would look into the matter and if she found anything questionable or illegal she would gain evidence for it, which Mrs Wilton could present to the county councillor, Mr Clayton.

"But I must state if I cannot find anything, I will not fabricate it and so we will just have to be satisfied that there may not be a solution to this problem."

"I am sure you will do a thorough job, as always, Clara, and I trust in you that you will find a way to resolve this."

Mrs Wilton's firm words did not inspire confidence in Clara. She did not like the idea that the woman would not take no for an answer.

Before Mrs Wilton left the office, she drew something out of her handbag and dropped it onto Clara's desk as if it were dirty and that she did not really wish to touch it.

"What is this?" Clara asked.

"A brochure for the Sun Club," Mrs Wilton shuddered as she spoke of it. "Edward gave it to me. I think you'll find more use for it than I do. I do not want the ghastly thing in my house."

With that final statement, Mrs Wilton left the office, leaving Clara wondering just precisely what she was going to do and how on earth she was going to infiltrate the Sun Club without having to risk taking off her clothes.

Chapter Three

Tommy had decided to take the dogs on an extra-long walk that morning. It was a fine, crisp early October day. The sun still had some strength to it, and the leaves, though they were turning a beautiful orange shade, still clung to the trees tenaciously. He decided to take the dogs out into the countryside on a route he didn't walk very often, but which he knew would take them through a nice area of woodland. It was a little bit of a hike to get there, but once he arrived he was glad he had made the decision. Pip and Bramble looked ecstatic to be wandering somewhere new.

Pip barrelled along through the bracken and brush between the trees, behaving like the working Labrador she was, and looking for a bird she could pick up or flush. Bramble tried to keep pace; being much smaller and a curly poodle, he bounced along, becoming indignant when Pip's charging around threw leaves upon him, or he got his coat tangled on the occasional thorn. Tommy had to rescue him repeatedly. The happiness they both displayed being able to run freely about cheered Tommy to his heart. He walked along slowly behind them, occasionally kicking up loose leaves and smiling to himself in that way that only comes from watching a dog play around so merrily. Everything felt good in the world that day. He started to whistle to himself, hands in his pocket as he glanced up towards the blue sky and contemplated how they were heading back into winter again. Yet, when the sun warmed you, you could still suppose you were clinging to the last dregs of a late summer.

There was a footpath that wound through the forest and ran for a stretch alongside a stone wall. He followed it and found himself beside a field where cattle were quietly grazing. Tommy admired the robust animals. They were bullocks being prepared for the beef market and were large, stocky animals. The sort that could certainly trample a man or a dog with ease, though by and large cattle were more curious than they were aggressive. If you treated them the right way, you were usually pretty safe, not that Tommy was going to risk anything, such as climbing into the field.

He had reached the corner of the field where the footpath turned back into the woodland, when he spied a man sitting on the wall and gazing out into the distance. From the look of his clothes, he must be a farm worker but, worryingly, he had a shotgun nestled in the crook of his arm. It was currently broken open so could not be used, but it would only take a second to slap the barrel back into place and point it at anybody or any dog. A sense of unease came over Tommy. His dogs were causing no problem but that did not always mean people took kindly to their presence. He called Pip and Bramble to him and had them slip into a heel position beside him, even though Bramble looked displeased at such a request.

The person on the wall had spotted them. He looked up and nodded in a friendly manner at Tommy, indicating that he was not concerned about his presence nor the dogs.

"Nice Labrador," he called out.

With this reassurance, Tommy allowed the dogs to start mooching around again and wandered over to the fellow to have a chat. The farm worker seemed interested in speaking to him. He was aged somewhere in his thirties, wearing the shabby, well-worn clothes of a labourer. His trousers had been often repaired and the cuffs around his ankles had been tied tightly around his legs with string, presumably to stop anything from climbing into them. His boots were muddy but serviceable. His tweed jacket was worn shiny in places. Yet he gave the overall impression of being well turned out, as if he had done his best with what he had.

Tommy noted the gentleman also looked bored and suspected he was keen enough to have a chat.

"Good morning," Tommy said. "Why are you sitting there with a shotgun?"

The fellow gave him a broad grin, revealing a couple of missing teeth.

"I am protecting the cattle," he said. "Never thought I would say such a thing. Feels like something you'd read about in one of those books about Cowboys. You know, when they have cattle rustlers they have to scare away from the ranch."

Tommy did not read much cowboy fiction, but he did know that this was just the sort of thing that cowboys were supposed to do.

"I did not know cattle rustling was a problem in Brighton," Tommy remarked.

"Oh, it's not," the labourer responded. "I was just merely saying how it made me feel like I was in those wild west books, you know. I always say to my missus, it is the one thing that makes me glad I learned to read that I can enjoy those cowboy books. I like to imagine what it must have been like to be out there. Herding up the cattle on backs of horses, roaming over such vast distances."

"Being shot at," Tommy said ironically, nodding towards the shotgun in the man's hands.

The labourer laughed.

"Well, I suppose this does look peculiar, but this has nothing to do with cattle rustling or me trying to be a cowboy. In fact, I would much rather be getting on with my usual work. But old man Franklin – he would be the farmer who owns these cattle – he says to me, 'Jasper, get yourself a shotgun and go sit up on that wall at the top field and watch them cattle and I don't want you moving all day. Someone will bring you some lunch and some cider when the time comes.' And I say to him, 'well, what do I do when night comes? Am I to leave then?' And he says, 'you will leave, but someone will be replacing you. And you mustn't take the shotgun with you.'"

Tommy frowned at this statement.

"Why has he got you sitting up here guarding the cattle with a shotgun if there aren't cattle rustlers around?"

"I didn't explain myself well," Jasper nodded. "You see, it's all to do with that thing old man Franklin saw in the newspaper this morning. He read it out loud to all of us while we were stood in the stockyard. There's a notice to say that a bear is on the loose."

"A bear?" Tommy said, thinking to himself that he had failed to get a newspaper that morning.

"That's right, a bear," Jasper said firmly. "Old man Franklin, he says, 'I'm not losing any of my bullocks to a bear, so you better go up there, Jasper, and you sit on that wall, and you watch them.' Well, I'm bored stiff and nothing's come along aside from you and them two dogs. Nothing that looks like a bear, anyway."

"Where has this bear come from?" Tommy asked, curious.

"The paper didn't say much, just that it's escaped from some private collector's menagerie and was on the loose. You know what these fancy people are like. They have all this money, and they don't know what to do with it. So, they buy some exotic animal and house it in a way that it can escape and wreak havoc on the general public."

"And has this bear been wreaking havoc?" Tommy asked.

"Couldn't say," Jasper replied. "It didn't mention it in the article. But old man Franklin, he says he don't want to risk his cattle, and I don't blame him. These bullocks are not far off from going to slaughter, and they'll bring in a good price. I'm thinking if I do a good job looking over them, I might get a bonus before Christmas, and won't that please the wife?

Tommy imagined that would please anyone a good deal.

"A bear," he said, glancing now into the forest where the dogs had disappeared into the undergrowth. He felt a pang of anxiety and wondered if he should call them back.

"That's right, a bear," Jasper replied. "I saw a stuffed one once, in one of those fairground attractions. It was standing up on its rear legs, and it was as tall as a man. If I see one of them things coming towards the cattle, I'll shoot first and ask questions later."

Tommy found himself itching to get out of the forest. It no longer felt the peaceful, happy place it had been. He was starting to think that it was a very good area for a bear to be roaming. He said his farewells to Jasper, wished him well in his bear hunting and headed off after the dogs as fast as he could. He rounded them up and curtailed their walk early, heading back towards town and thinking to himself he would collect the newspaper on his way home just to see if what he had been told was accurate. If it was, he might just have to mention to Annie about making sure her chickens were safe.

Chapter Four

C lara had a luncheon appointment with Captain O'Harris. O'Harris was her fiancé and ran a home for the recuperation of men who had served in the Great War. They did not spend as much time together as Clara would like. There always seemed to be something getting in the way, and they were trying to make amends for that by regularly meeting up. They also had a lot to discuss, for their wedding plans seemed to be getting stuck in a similar cycle of indecision. They couldn't decide where to get married, when, or even what exactly they would like for their ceremony and the event afterwards. As much as Clara craved something simple, and O'Harris was quite in agreement, they both knew that Annie would be looking forward to something far more decadent. If Annie suggested she was going to make the wedding cake, as she had attempted to do for her own wedding, Clara may have to throw her hands up in despair. She could not go through that trauma yet again.

She arrived at the Home and was greeted warmly by a couple of the soldiers; they were all familiar with Clara and knew her as a friendly face. They immediately asked about Annie, because Annie often taught them home economics classes, everything from baking to sewing. She taught the men, believing that they needed to know these skills, just as any woman did. Some of the men – who were almost all from the officer ranks – had been quite reluctant to take part in these classes initially, but Annie brooked no argument and routinely made sure to dispel such notions that baking and sewing were women's work alone. The men needed to be independent. They needed to be able to sort themselves out, and learning these skills gave them a newfound sense of wholeness. The simplicity of baking a cake, as Annie pointed out, could be very healing.

Clara found O'Harris in his office. He rose from behind a desk loaded with paperwork and raced towards her. He put his arms around her and hugged her tight, and she hugged him back. Then he leaned forward and kissed first her forehead, then both her cheeks. Clara grinned at him, stepped back and then reached forward and kissed him firmly on the lips.

"All right, all right," O'Harris said with a chuckle after they had kissed. "I know I agreed to stop with being so formal, but I still can't quite get used to the idea of kissing you on the mouth."

"You need to get used to it. We are going to be married soon enough and then things are going to get very interesting."

"Now don't tease and torment me, Clara. I can't wait until we are properly husband and wife and can do all the things we wish to do."

"I hope you don't mean working on all my cases together," Clara said, jesting.

"Naturally, that is the only thing I have on my mind!" O'Harris laughed. "Are you hungry? I have had the cook prepare us a luncheon all to ourselves."

"I am hungry," Clara agreed. "And I have something interesting for us to peruse while we eat."

She showed him the brochure that Mrs Wilton had left behind. O'Harris raised an eyebrow. The imagery on the front cover was very discreet and subtle. Nothing inappropriate was being shown. However, it was still clear that the brochure was about people walking around naked.

"If you were considering this for our honeymoon, I am not sure I'm quite ready for such a step," O'Harris said.

"Come now, I quite want to see you with your clothes off," Clara grinned at him.

"Miss Fitzgerald, that is quite risqué of you," O'Harris feigned shock.

Clara chuckled at him. O'Harris leaned down and whispered in her ear.

"Quite often, dear Clara, all I find myself thinking about is you without any clothes on."

Clara blushed, though not from embarrassment.

"We ought to get a move on with this wedding, don't you think? Before we can control ourselves no longer."

"I am wholly in agreement," O'Harris drew her close again. "What about we elope tomorrow?"

"Sounds perfect. You can tell Annie."

The thought of Annie's wrath and displeasure was enough to still any man's ardour.

"I think we better go to luncheon before we do something rash," O'Harris said firmly. "Why are you carrying a rather provocative brochure if not for our honeymoon?"

"It is most certainly not for our honeymoon. I do not intend to share you with anybody else, and certainly I have no intention of allowing other young ladies to see you unclad. You are attractive enough to them as it is. I would never get them away from you."

"Think you might be overestimating my appeal to women," O'Harris chuckled.

"And you are forgetting what a handsome former RFC officer you are. After all, that is why I fell for you."

"That and my charming manners," O'Harris pointed out. "And the fact I can drive a car."

"Well, precisely. The car was certainly a clincher."

Still laughing they headed through to O'Harris' private dining room, where their was food being brought to the table. It smelt delicious; the cook had created a dish of chicken and mushrooms served with seasonal vegetables and a creamy sauce. Clara had not realised quite how hungry she was until she entered the room and suddenly felt her mouth watering. Her stomach gave a rebuking rumble.

"I shall never have the svelte waistline that is fashionable with all this food before me, and with the size of my appetite," she sighed to herself.

"I jolly well hope you never do have such a waistline," O'Harris told her. "Those waif-like girls have never appealed to me. You are a proper woman, Clara, with all the curves in all the right places. And if that is too forward a thing to say, I do not care."

"And that, Captain O'Harris, is exactly why I am marrying you."

"Because I am forward?"

"Because you love me for exactly who I am," Clara smiled. "I could not have asked for more."

They started to eat, but before long, conversation turned around to the brochure that Clara had left half concealed under a teacup. O'Harris found his eyes kept flicking to the front cover, which was black and white, and showed a very discreet few of people sitting in deck chairs. From the angle of the camera, and the fact that you were behind the sitters, it was only possible to see their bare legs and shoulders, but it was quite plain that everyone was stark naked.

"What is this all about then?" He asked, jabbing a knife at the brochure.

"The Brighton Sun Club," Clara explained. "It has just started up and has its own section of private beach. Mrs Wilton is utterly appalled and wants me to investigate and find out if they are doing anything improper that could force the council to shut them down."

"Why is Mrs Wilton so up in arms?"

"Firstly, the private beach is not so far from her own home, and she has a terrible fear that she might accidentally look upon a naked man at some point. Secondly, her son Edward has announced his intention of joining the Sun Club."

"Oh," O'Harris said, seeing precisely why Mrs Wilton might be so upset. "But you turned her down, I suppose.

"It was easier to agree to it. You know what she's like."

"But if you go there and they are following all the things that they're supposed to do, and fulfilling all the legal requirements, you're just going to have to tell her that you've wasted her money."

"I know that, and I explained that to Mrs Wilton, but what am I going to do? She won't give up on this notion until I can prove something. I have considered having a word with Edward, seeing if he is willing to pretend that he's no longer part of the Sun Club."

"That might be the simplest solution. When the news of this place spreads around Brighton, I have no doubt there will be plenty of others who will have something to say about it. Things like this have a tendency to bring out the worst in people. You might as well tell them they're opening a new brothel on the High Street."

"I agree. People are going to see this and take it as an affront to their principles and morals. There will be quite an outpouring of disgust and hatred. But no doubt those who are in charge of the Sun Club have already considered that. I have glanced through the brochure and there seem to be a variety of restrictions in place. Which will make it not only a safe place for the residents but should appease anyone who is concerned about the improprieties that might be going on."

"What sort of restrictions?" O'Harris asked.

"For a start, male members must be accompanied by a female, preferably their wife, though it does not state that a man has to be married to go there. It is made plain that casual relationships between guests are banned. You turn up with the person you intend to be spending the holiday with, and you remain with that person. Secondly, all the members go under pseudonyms so as to avoid being recognised in everyday life. They refer to these as club names.

"Another restriction is that nobody is allowed to wear jewellery and that sandals ought to be worn when indoors, and towels have to be placed on furniture when anybody sits down for hygiene reasons. Finally, no one is allowed to give a compliment on someone else's appearance. I suppose that is to try and avoid things such as flirting or accusations of sexual harassment."

"But people are still going around naked with one another?" O'Harris said, scratching at his chin and thinking about this.

"Why should that make things so different to going around with people with their clothes on? After all, are we so corrupt that the second someone has no clothes on, we suddenly consider them more attractive than when they are dressed, and that will change our behaviour towards them?"

"I Imagine that is one of the principles that the naturist movement would discuss. The fact that it's not about the people being naked, that makes them sexualized. It's about a person's attitude to the other people, and that attitude could come across even if they were wearing clothes. The problem is you have to be pretty high minded to see things like that. Most people in Brighton are only going to see what is right before them."

O'Harris stifled a smirk.

"And that is naked people. That is what is right before them."

"Precisely," Clara groaned. "Well, I shall do what I can to appease Mrs Wilton. Beyond that, I don't intend to take it any further."

"If male members can only join this club and attend if they have a female companion, precisely who is Edward going with?" O'Harris remarked. "I was under the impression he had not married yet."

"You are correct. As far as I am aware, Edward is still a bachelor, but I suppose he may have found himself a willing friend to accompany him. I don't imagine he stated *that* to his mother."

"But he gave her this brochure to look through."

"Edward would have been fully confident that his mother would not look through that brochure in case she risked seeing something she did not care to see."

"If you are going on this adventure, you are going to need a companion to go with you," O'Harris pointed out.

"I have no intention of joining the Sun Club," Clara remarked.

"But the rules state you have to go in pairs to enter it. Come on Clara, you have to let me come along for the ride on this one."

"I thought you said you only had eyes for me," Clara pretended to be offended.

"Naturally... I mean, it's only out of curiosity after all."

She let him squirm for a moment, looking uncomfortable and not sure how to explain himself, then she chuckled.

"I could hardly wave this in front of you, then refuse to let you come," she smiled. "I think it certainly could be an entertaining adventure. Of course, we are assuming that all the people who wish to disrobe at the Sun Club are the sort of people to have glamorous figures."

"You mean they could all be people in their sixties who have let themselves go?"

"Precisely," Clara grinned.

Chapter Five

Tommy had picked up a copy of the newspaper and he had trawled through it to find the very small announcement that a brown bear was missing from a private collection. The notice was so small it was almost as if it had been placed as an afterthought.

The notification also did not state where the bear had been lost. So, it was difficult to say where it would be appropriate to look. It was more an item of slight interest to fill space in the *Brighton Gazette*. One had to assume the bear was missing in the area, yet it could easily be missing in Hove or further afield. Tommy decided that old man Franklin's fears for his cattle were probably unfounded. He was also not sure if bears regularly went out and killed such large animals, when there was probably plenty of other food around that was easier to target. Such as sheep, chickens, and the wildlife in the countryside. Not to mention he was sure he had read that bears were natural scavengers and would quite happily raid rubbish bins.

He decided not to mention the situation to Annie, after all. Just in case she became overly concerned for her chickens. She might insist on bringing them in at night to their bedroom, where she could keep a firm eye on them, and the last thing he desired was to be lying in bed and hearing the hens clucking from their box. It would put a man off other things.

Unfortunately for Tommy, he should have realised that the gossip grapevine within Brighton was far more powerful than his intentions to keep Annie in the dark. He had barely walked into the house when she rushed up to him, threw her arms around him and almost yelled into his ear.

"I am so relieved you are home. I was so concerned about you."

"Whatever for?" Tommy asked in astonishment.

"Haven't you heard?" Annie was about to say more when she noted the newspaper in his hand. "Well, you've got a copy of the paper. Surely you have read about it?"

Tommy did not want to admit that he had read about the bear, just in case there was something else Annie was referring to.

"I have glanced at it, but I haven't read it thoroughly yet."

"There is a bear on the loose!" Annie said, poking at the paper. "Jenny from two doors down, told me. In fact, all the girls in the neighbourhood know. We were discussing whether it will be safe to go out to do our household chores. Imagine going to the butchers and being jumped upon by a great big brown bear."

"Annie, I really do not think that brown bears go around jumping on people. Especially when they happen to be heading towards the butchers."

"How do you know what a brown bear might do if it was hungry enough?" Annie pointed out, folding her arms across her chest. Now she had stepped back and was giving Tommy a firm look. He knew that look and he also knew he was at risk of getting into trouble very rapidly.

"We can lock the chickens in the pantry," he said quickly, before she could suggest anything else. "Overnight, that is, just to be on the safe side. But I don't think you need to worry. I doubt the bear is actually in town. It will be somewhere out in the countryside."

"It almost sounds as though you have been considering this matter," Annie said calmly. "As if you already knew a bear was on the loose but had no intention of telling me."

"I saw no reason to get alarmed about it. It sounded just like some minor thing, probably it isn't even roaming the countryside. I don't see how it affects us."

"That is where you are wrong, because if there is a bear on the loose wandering round the town, the first place it will go is all the yards looking for food and then it will come after us. You are quite right; I will be putting my hens in the pantry overnight. In fact, maybe I should have them there during the day as well, just in case."

"I think that would be going too far," Tommy said quickly, remembering the mess that her hens had made last time they had to be kept in the pantry in an emergency. "I don't think bears go wandering around in broad daylight, and in any case, if we heard something in the back garden, we'd set Pip on it."

"You would set your dog on a brown bear," Annie glared at him.

Tommy knew he was on a sticky wicket now; there was absolutely no way that, firstly, he would put his own dog at risk and, secondly, that he would consider harming an animal that just happened to be roaming around.

"All right, I wouldn't do that. But we would do something. I think bears are scared by loud noises. Throwing some tins or something at it would probably send it running."

"Where have you heard that?" Annie asked him firmly.

"I'm sure I read it in a book, but my point is we don't have to panic. I very much doubt it's going to come anywhere near us."

"As far as I can see, the whole town is in a panic," Annie remarked. "Everyone I have spoken to is up in arms and wants to know what the police are doing about this. In fact, as soon as Clara is home, I'm going to ask her if she has spoken to Inspector Park-Coombs about this matter. He must have all his constables out searching for this dangerous animal."

"There was nothing in the paper to suggest that the animal was dangerous," Tommy said.

"That's typical newspaper talk for you, trying to keep things under wraps so that nobody is going to get panicky and start to ask why nothing is being done. I tell you, this bear needs to be caught sooner rather than later."

Annie hammered her fist into an open palm to emphasise her point.

"I'm sure everything will be just fine," Tommy was saying before he was interrupted by a sudden cry from the kitchen.

Annie headed from the hallway back to her own private domain. Stood in the outside doorway was a young woman wearing a maid's uniform, and presumably from one of the houses down the row.

"Ethel!" Annie shouted in alarm, seeing the girl's fraught expression. "What has happened?"

"We've seen the bear, Annie," the girl echoed. "It's currently in Mrs Broome's back garden rummaging around behind the compost heap that Mr Broome put up. I came running for you at once because none of us knows what to do."

"See?" Annie said, turning on her husband and glaring at him. "This is exactly what I was talking about. Now what shall we do about all this, Mr Clever Clogs? Where are those tins you suggested rattling?"

Tommy knew Annie was not in a good mood to be teased at this point, and it was best not to argue with her, especially if he wanted some dinner later on.

"I shall come take a look myself," he told Ethel. "Lead the way."

Ethel did lead the way out through their back garden and along the alley that ran behind, towards the garden of the Broome household. Annie followed behind Tommy. Her footsteps seemed to be clacking louder than normal, as if she were making a point with every step. He didn't dare look over his shoulder, because he was sure her arms were crossed across her chest, and she was glowering at him. He tried to remain calm, reminding himself there could not possibly be a bear wandering around in the Broome's back garden.

There were a gaggle of girls outside the garden gate. They were all hovering there, speaking in hushed whispers.

"Where precisely are the Broomes?" Tommy asked when he turned up.

Three eager faces turned up to him. The girls were all young and a little foolish, the sight of a man turning up to rescue them drew a collective sigh of relief. Tommy reflected that Clara would disapprove of girls behaving in such a manner. She considered that women should be able to sort out their own problems for themselves, and she certainly wouldn't have gone off to fetch a man to resolve an issue with the bear. Unless she desperately needed to.

"They are away visiting their daughter," Ethel told him. "There is no one in the house but we saw the bear over the fence, and we can hear it snuffling about."

Tommy went to open the gate and Annie caught his arm.

"Maybe you should just look over the fence first?" She suggested, showing the first sign of actual concern.

Tommy hoisted himself up so he could see over the fence. He could spy the compost heap which was situated just beside the garden shed and he could also hear a sniffling noise and see something brown rummaging around in the gap where the compost heap sat next to the wall of the shed. Whatever was there, it did look quite big, though he could not say for certain it was a bear. Just in that instant, he had a pang of unease. What was he supposed to do if it was the creature?

He did something that he would not normally admit to doing. He asked himself, what would Clara do? This question, which sometimes popped into his head, usually gave him a solution. Not one that he would always pick, but usually one that worked out, nonetheless. He decided that Clara would stroll straight into the back garden, fully committed to the idea that there could not possibly be a bear there.

That was exactly what he did. He could hear the girls behind him saying in hushed tones that he must not go in, even as he walked forward. He closed the gate behind him and picked up the first thing that came to hand, which was a garden hoe that had been left out in the rain. The handle had started to splinter, and it was sharp under his grip. He walked towards the animal that was rummaging in the compost heap. When he was a few feet away he banged the hoe against the garden path to make a noise.

The creature, rummaging in the compost bin, paused. Tommy held his breath. He reached out and banged the hoe yet again. Suddenly, from the compost heap, the creature sprang straight in his direction, and he gave out a voluble shout, thinking he was about to be savaged by something large. Annie burst through the garden gate, determined to come to his aid, in time to see the largest cat she had ever known, running past her and up over the fence to get away from them. It was not clear who looked more sheepish; Tommy for shouting or Annie for believing the bear was in the back garden, or Ethel and the other girls for announcing it was there in the first place. It was all agreed that no one would say any more on the matter and they would pretend it hadn't happened. Returning the hoe to where he had discovered it, Tommy and Annie walked back to their house.

"You see how people get hysterical about nothing?" Tommy grumbled. He had fallen back hard when he had jumped away from the cat and had grazed his hand.

Annie muttered something under her breath but refused to say anything more about it.

Chapter Six

C lara considered it prudent to make an appointment to go and visit the Sun Club the following day. She felt arriving unannounced to somewhere such as a nudist camp was an unwise idea. For a start, she was not entirely sure what she might witness. Clara was far from squeamish, and certainly not prudish, at least not compared to a good deal of people. But the thought of seeing random individuals unclad gave her the chills. Precisely who might she come across at the nudist camp suddenly bare skinned? What if it was the mayor?

She had had a horrible dream the previous night concerning Inspector Park-Coombs and the possibility that he had suddenly decided to become a member of the nudist camp. It was an image she did not care for, and one that would take a considerable amount of time to get out of her head. She wondered how she would ever be able to look the inspector in the eyes again.

It was easy enough to get in touch with the Sun Club. The owner was a lady who went by the name of Miss Daisy Belle. Clara was not sure if this was her actual name, or one she had taken up to mask her own identity, like those who attended the nudist camp.

Miss Belle was quite happy for Clara to come and visit her. She always welcomed inquiring minds. Those who were prepared to look beyond the narrow prejudices of society and see things for themselves. Clara possibly had laid it on a bit thick when she had suggested that she was inclined towards the naturist movement and wanted to understand it better, rather than to listen to the local gossip. But such subterfuge seemed necessary to get Miss Belle on her side.

Clara intended to make this first rendezvous alone, despite her promise to O'Harris. When she mentioned the meeting to Tommy he was aghast.

"Did you say it's a camp where everybody wears no clothes?" He repeated at least three times before he could believe what Clara had told him.

They were having the conversation down the bottom of the garden under the pretence of looking for possible ways a bear could enter and get at the chickens. This was both to appease Annie and to make sure they were well away from her when Clara mentioned words such as nudist, naked, unclad, and so forth. Annie's views on such matters were not best repeated. Annie was quite old fashioned in many regards, and she would certainly be appalled at the thought of either of them going to such a place. She no doubt would have visions of Clara casting off all her clothes and running around freely on the grass, as if she suddenly would lose all sense of propriety the second she arrived there.

"You cannot possibly think it's a good idea," Tommy said to her.

"Do you mean going to speak to Miss Belle or the nudist camp as a whole?" Clara asked him.

"Both. I mean, you might see men who have no clothes on."

"Well, it's a little bit nippy today, so I'm not particularly worried about that. My understanding from Miss Belle is the club is opening this late in the season not to expect customers, but rather to get people gradually used to the idea before they welcome visitors properly next season."

"And that's exactly the point. *Get people used to the idea*. Clearly she knows it's controversial. It's scandalous."

"Miss Belle was very quick to point out it had nothing to do with sexualizing the human body. It is not a brothel or a club where people can go and find partners for irresponsible behaviour. Guests have to arrive as couples, and they're not allowed to swap their partners."

"What do you mean swap their partners?"

Clara eyed up her brother, knowing that he was fully aware of what she meant, but was deciding to push the issue.

"It is not a sex club," she said carefully. "My understanding is that it is more about being at one with nature and appreciating the human body. Miss Belle made it very clear that most of her members are actually very private and innocent in that regard."

"She can say that as much as she likes, doesn't mean it's true."

"Well, the point is she's not breaking any laws and I promised Mrs Wilton I would go see what was going on. I dare say all I will end up doing is finding out more information to prove that everything is above board. But Mrs Wilton is quite glad to pay me for the matter."

"Could you not just speak to her son and suggest he doesn't carry on with the club?" Tommy suggested. "That would be easier for everyone."

"It would be easier for Mrs Wilton, perhaps. But who's to say he doesn't actually believe in this place? My understanding is that Edward has become rather lost since the war. I am also somewhat curious as to who is accompanying him to the club, for he cannot attend alone."

"He is not married," Tommy remembered. "Which makes his attendance of the club with a female companion even more scandalous."

"I rather think the word scandalous is used far too often," Clara told him firmly. "And used inappropriately. After all, what does it matter to me or you what Edward is doing with his lady companion, as long as he treats her decently and understands that any consequences are as much his responsibility as hers?"

"Sometimes you are far too liberal, Clara," Tommy folded his arms and stared at her.

"We're striding into a new century," Clara told him. "However, I will admit I am not inclined to see a load of people naked who I do not know. There is only one person who I would ever care to see naked…"

Clara realised her slip as it exited her mouth and gasped. She had not meant to be so revealing.

Tommy chuckled.

"Should I start preparing O Harris for his membership to the Sun Club?" He said with a grin.

"You will not mention any of that," Clara glared at him.

Still laughing heartily, Tommy got out of his sister's way and allowed her to carry on with her mission for the day. Since she was not going to take Captain O'Harris on this first visit, (feeling Miss Belle might be more open to speaking to her if she went alone) she would have to make her way by bus. Miss Belle had suggested the best route for her to take to get her within easy walking distance of the Sun Club. The entranceway was apparently quite difficult to find, deliberately so, so that people couldn't accidentally come upon it. Miss Belle had hinted there had already been some trouble with people protesting what she was about. At the same time, she was not inclined to be worried about it. Her estate was very private, well fenced and the gates secure. Anyone who managed to get in unauthorised would be trespassing.

In some regards, Clara realised she was quite privileged to be allowed to enter the place considering she was quite the outsider. She suspected, after talking with Miss Belle for a while, that the woman had heard her name before and knew exactly who she was.

Sometimes Clara's reputation could work in her favour.

Leaving Tommy behind to continue his bear hunt, Clara headed out and caught the first bus.

It required three changes of bus to get her to the lane that would enable her to reach the Sun Club. She was under the impression that most people did not travel by bus to reach it; that those who could afford membership could also afford a vehicle.

Precisely where Edward was getting the money to afford to be at the Sun Club was an interesting question. One of many she hoped to answer that day. But first off, she had to walk down the lane, find the gates, and get in. The gates, as Miss Belle had told her, were locked. There was a gatekeeper who answered Clara's knock and when he heard her name nodded that she could come in.

"Miss Belle is expecting you," he said. "Head straight down to the house and knock on the door."

Clara would have liked to have asked him what his thoughts were on the Sun Club and how he came to have a position there. Being the gatekeeper, he was fully clad and wrapped up well for the weather, which had started to turn chilly.

Clara did not ask. Instead, she set off towards the house. Keeping her eyes straight ahead just in case she saw some random naked people running across the lawn.

Chapter Seven

C lara discovered the front door was also locked. She knocked
and then, just in case, rang an old-fashioned bell that was beside
the door and had a circular handle on a chain. You pulled it straight
down and somewhere deep in the house a bell rang in a jolly fashion.
It was not long before someone came and turned the lock on the door
to open it. The woman before Clara, who she assumed was Miss Daisy
Belle, was younger than she had anticipated. Somehow, in her mind,
Clara had supposed that the person who would organise and run a
nudist camp would be relatively mature. Miss Belle was somewhere
in her early 30s. Her hair hung loose down her back and around her
shoulders. She wore a plain skirt, a knitted cardigan, and a blouse with
tiny white flowers upon it. On her feet were a pair of tartan slippers.
She did not strike Clara as a person who would go cavorting about on
the beach without any clothes on. She stared at Clara with the palest
blue eyes she had seen in a long time. So pale, in fact, that with the
pupils small in the light of day, they almost seemed to vanish. It was
an icy, somehow disturbing stare.

"You must be Miss Fitzgerald," Miss Belle said, emphasising the
title just a fraction.

Clara got the impression that Miss Belle was very precious about the fact that she was not married. That she was disinclined to such an institution and would gladly tell anybody about it.

"I am," Clara said, holding out her hand for Miss Belle to shake.

It was a pointed gesture to demonstrate that Clara was a forward-thinking woman who appreciated other forward-thinking women and was quite inclined to encourage those who wished to set up in business themselves. A hint of a smile curled the edges of Miss Belle's lips as she saw the offered hand. She took it and shook heartily.

"Come into the drawing room," she said. "I have got the tea things ready and there is some ginger cake. You must be hungry after all the travelling you did to get here."

Clara confessed that jumping between three buses had certainly been taxing, if not particularly tiring. She was quite glad to get into the drawing room, which had a fire burning in the fireplace that took the edge off the autumn weather. It was not yet cold, but there was a dampness about everything. Sometimes, if you found yourself in a patch of sunlight, it could almost feel as warm as summer, then the next moment a cloud would pass across and you would find yourself shivering.

"Not quite the season for discarding one's clothes just yet," Clara remarked.

"Were you expecting to see people running around nude on the lawn?" Miss Belle chuckled. "No, that is not how we do things. There is a private beach where people can sunbathe naked, of course. And there are specific areas in the house where everyone can go around naked. But the front lawn is off limits in that regard. For the safety of my guests, and for our privacy to avoid those who might try and catch a glance over the fence."

"You appear to have thought of everything," Clara observed.

"One must when one knows that what they are doing is going

to cause a scandal. I do detest that word, what a load of nonsense for people just behaving as God intended. We are not a brothel or anything of that description. We do not even have an alcohol licence. I refuse to have alcohol on the site and certainly not drugs. This is a place for people to commune with nature, for people who do not wish to go around wearing clothes. It's about freedom, freedom of the spirit. Unfortunately, there are others who cannot see it that way. They are narrow minded. They think that the human body is only designed for one thing and that it must be shrouded in cloth to protect us from our rampant carnal desires. It is sad to suppose there are those who think we cannot have evolved beyond such base instincts."

"The world is a complicated place," Clara said. "And to be fair, people have seen far too much of the dark side of it lately. It rather tarnishes their view."

"Well, they need to start lifting their heads up and seeing it for what it is. The beauty of the actual world. The beauty of the human body. But there we go, Miss Fitzgerald. The very fact you are here suggests to me that you understand this to a degree and that you are prepared to listen."

"I am certainly willing to hear your point of view," Clara replied. "I won't lie and say that I'm entirely comfortable with what is happening here, and in fact I had a terrible thought about what might happen if I saw someone I knew without their clothes on."

"That is exactly my point. Why should it matter if someone is clad or not? What is so wrong about the human body that we must mask it over? Oh, I know what people say. It is all to do with the genitals. That the mere sight of them will inflame desire in all but the most prudish of persons. It really does make you despair about human nature, if that is all we come down to. You know there are societies in other parts of the world where people do not go around routinely wearing clothes? And in those societies rampant orgies are not occurring every second of the day. Those people behave quite sophisticatedly and civilised among one another."

Clara wondered what people she was referring to who went around completely naked all the time. As far as she was aware, even societies where clothing was limited, something was usually worn around the waists and hips. She decided not to argue with the woman.

"I am afraid to say I have had some people suggesting to me that I should come here and inspect the Sun Club with the purpose of shutting you down," she told Miss Belle honestly. "I do not agree with them. If you are not breaking any rules and everybody is being responsible here, then it is not up to me or anyone else to determine if what you are doing is wrong. If you are not harming each other or harming anyone else, then I say you are quite welcome to do as you please, even if it is perhaps not my cup of tea."

"A very wise and, may I say, bold stance, Miss Fitzgerald," Miss Belle replied. "I admire a woman who speaks so clearly and soundly, and who does not allow silly prejudices to blind her. I am very willing to show you around our facilities and explain our rules so that you may respond to anyone who asks you about this place that it is perfectly above board."

"That sounds perfectly reasonable. I must assure you I have no intention of causing you trouble. The only reason I really came is because a friend of mine is somewhat concerned, and I felt that if I did nothing then she would certainly start causing you a great deal of bother."

"Now I am curious," Miss Belle said. "Who might be this friend of yours?"

Clara saw no reason to hide who had sent her.

"My friend's name is Mrs Wilton. I believe you know her son,

Edward."

Miss Belle gave a strange smirk.

"Oh, I know Edward very well," she said. "He helped me establish the Sun Club."

Clara had been about to take a sip of tea. The information caused her to start just a fraction and the teacup spilled some of its contents into the saucer. She was mildly embarrassed that she had reacted in this way. It had been one thing to think that Edward was attending the club as a member, and quite another to suppose that he was a co-founder. She started to wonder how on earth she would break that news to Mrs Wilton.

"I see that is something of a revelation to you," Miss Belle continued to smile.

"It is indeed, and I dare say his mother is going to get quite a shock when she hears it."

"I think Edward would prefer it if you allowed him to reveal that information at a time when he considers it appropriate."

"Of course, you are quite right," Clara nodded. "It is not my place to interfere in their relationship. I presume he is going to tell his mother?"

"I imagine he intends to, eventually, right now I think he is just more interested in getting this place up and running."

Clara sipped at her tea, trying to fathom what to ask next. Her mind had been rather thrown out by the information that Edward was behind the Sun Club. Miss Belle offered her a biscuit and a piece of ginger cake, which helped to delay her from having to ask anything more. It was, in fact, Miss Belle who spoke first.

"Would you care for a tour of the facilities?"

Clara was not sure how to reply.

"Do you have any guests present?"

"We do have a handful," Miss Belle smiled. "Though the weather is on the turn, it is still feasible for people to go around unclad. You get used to the cold when you go around for great deals of time unclothed. Couple more weeks and it will all change but I do believe there are people at this moment down on the sea bathing. I must state firmly Miss Fitzgerald that my guests are not here to be gawped at. They are not some attraction, but they will not be fussed if we wander around and view the facilities while they go about their business. Just like any other tourist going about their business."

Clara did not know what to say, yet she also knew this was a test from Miss Belle to see just how far Clara's open mindedness went. She could have backed out there and then, she could have expressed her need to be somewhere else, that she had got all the information she wanted. Miss Belle had laid down a challenge to her, and Clara was not one to shirk a challenge easily.

"I would be delighted to take a tour of your camp," Clara told Miss Belle.

Miss Belle cast her an odd look. She seemed satisfied that Clara had agreed to take up the gauntlet.

"You are truly prepared for seeing everything?" She asked, just to be clear.

"I would be delighted to see everything," Clara told her firmly. "Do not feel you have to place limitations on where you take me."

They stared at each other. Warriors sizing each other up. Seeing which one would blink first.

"I think I'm going to like you, Miss Fitzgerald," Miss Belle stated.

Secretly, Clara fancied she was going to like Miss Belle too.

Chapter Eight

M iss Belle began the tour by taking Clara around the front rooms of the house, which she explained, were clothed-only areas. These included her office and the drawing room where she received visitors. It was also where the reception was for new arrivals. The front lawns, as she had already mentioned, were also off limits to anyone who was not clad in clothing.

"Purely for practical reasons," she explained to Clara. "We will have non-club visitors from time to time, and even some guests who are visiting for the first time may find it uncomfortable to see people fully naked on the lawns. As I mentioned before, I also don't want unwelcome visitors popping their heads over the front fencing and staring at my guests. There is a private garden at the back of the house, with tennis courts and other facilities, where my guests can roam around freely and without clothing."

The house tour was much as Clara would have expected. There was a library and a games room, a private sitting room, and a dining room. And of course, though she didn't take her to them, Miss Belle assured her there were fine kitchen facilities at the back where a handful of very carefully picked servants worked.

"They are always clothed," she told Clara. "For hygiene purposes."

She then took Clara upstairs and showed her around some of the guest bedrooms; the ones that were not currently being occupied. They were spacious and formed miniature suites, each having a bedroom and a bathroom. Miss Belle explained that there were also some luxury suites, which included a sitting room.

"You anticipate that your guests will be from the wealthier classes," Clara observed.

"I am afraid to say, Miss Fitzgerald, that when it comes to certain prejudices I am as affected as the next person. It is hard to imagine a working-class soul coming here and behaving themselves, for instance. I suppose, in some regards, I am no better than those who anticipate that all my guests are running around in a brothel I have set up."

Clara did not make any statement. In her experience, some of the worst for being prudish were those among the working classes. Despite generally being seen as lacking in manners, uncouth and unkempt, very often they were the ones that were the most old-fashioned in their attitudes. It was the upper classes who seemed to set out to scandalise everyone by doing things differently. Maybe it was something to do with the freedom that wealth gave a person. A working-class man or woman had to follow certain rules and restrictions to enable them to survive and keep working. They could not afford to behave in an odd or bizarre manner that could cause them to lose their income and home.

"What do you make of it so far?" Miss Belle said after they had completed the tour of the property.

"So far it seems to be like any other hotel I have come across within a stately home. It seems very luxurious and grand."

Miss Belle nodded.

"I must state that all the furniture requires people to place a towel upon it before they sit on it, unless they are clad or have underwear on," she continued. "It might sound odd but there are some limitations to what we do, and for hygiene reasons we must insist on that. The beds we are more flexible about because even in a regular hotel people might sleep in them without clothes on."

"Of course, you still have to consider these things."

"We're very generous with what we allow our guests, but there have to be some considerations for the well-being of others and to the continuation of this hotel. Not that we anticipate anything occurring of course, but well..."

Miss Belle tailed off and actually managed to blush under Clara's gaze. There proved to be some things that even she could be slightly embarrassed about.

"I shall show you our tennis court next," Miss Belle explained.

She headed off speedily, and Clara had to hurry to keep up. Clara's confidence was beginning to buckle as she thought about people playing tennis without any clothes on. More specifically, she found herself imagining what it would be like for her to play tennis naked. She didn't like the idea. She fancied there were a few too many soft parts of her body that would wobble like jelly as she jumped or lunged for the ball. Clara fancied that the whole point of clothing was to make the human body appear far more dignified than it really was. Unless you were particularly attractive, most people when they were not wearing clothes, were not terribly elegant. At least that was the way Clara thought, and maybe that in itself was an indication of her prejudices and how she had been brainwashed by society to view nudity as an embarrassing and ungainly thing.

She was thankful, nonetheless, that the tennis court was empty. Miss Belle then took them around some of the private gardens, showing them the lovely gazeboes and a small maze that was just beginning to grow up, and would be many years in the making, followed by a rose garden, though she did admit one had to be careful walking nude among roses.

They finally came to a pause in a herb garden where row upon rows of lavender bushes were growing and lightly scented the air. They were still just in bloom, though most of the flowers were beginning to die off. It had been a glorious September, and the lavender was clinging to that last bit of sun to make the most of it before it shut itself down for the winter.

"I shall now take you down to the beach. That is where we will find the guests today, I imagine," Miss Belle explained.

"How many guests do you have at the moment?"

"Seven. Quite a large number considering the time of year. You see, the naturist movement is very new in England and there aren't many places for those who wish to indulge in it to go. So, though I opened this place out of season, we already have some guests who wish to try it out and get a feel for it. They could not wait until next year."

A chilly autumnal wind then happened to blow past them, whipping at their skirts. Clara was trying to imagine what it would be like to be naked with that wind tickling around you. She didn't fancy it personally.

"What about you?" She asked Miss Belle.

"Do you mean, do I go around without any clothes on? Well, if that is your question, then I can assure you, yes I do. But I don't have the luxury of doing so very often. Like today, I had to greet you, of course. And when other guests are appearing, I will have to greet them clad as I said, at the front of the house. But when I get the opportunity, I do appreciate being able to strip everything off and live as nature intended."

Clara found herself coming very close to asking a similar question about Edward, and then caught herself. She didn't think it was really proper to ask if a young gentleman liked to go around without his clothes on, even in a nudist camp.

"Come along, I will take you down to the beach. There is a steep set of stairs in the cliff but they're not so bad to walk down. Are you quite ready?"

There had been a slight edge to the last statement, and Clara knew exactly what Miss Belle meant by it. Clara doubted she could ever be fully ready for what she was about to see but she refused to be intimidated or to allow Miss Belle to see that she was concerned.

"I am quite ready, Miss Belle," she told her. "Lead on."

Miss Belle took them to the edge of the gardens and showed Clara down a set of stairs that were indeed slightly steep. Fortunately, they were dry and free from anything that could cause them to be slippery. Clara kept her head down for a while, not wishing to look up and spy anybody on the beach. It wasn't so much that she now was concerned about seeing someone naked, more that she felt as if she was spying on them, and that she was being rude. But as she got to the last third of the staircase, she found her curiosity getting the better of her and, without really realising it, she lifted her eyes up and looked out across the sand. She saw several heads bobbing about in the sea and that was it. There was no sign of naked bodies. She breathed a short sigh of relief. Miss Belle heard her and turned her head, recognising the gesture and amused by it.

"I am always amazed at how people worry so much about seeing someone else naked," she remarked. "Even my guests who come here with the purpose of taking off their clothes can be a little sheepish about seeing someone else unclad."

"And they must not compliment each other?" Clara asked.

"That is absolutely the case. You must not say to someone else that you believe them to be particularly handsome or beautiful, or to admire their body. It is one of the rules we have in place to stop any improper behaviour occurring. Also, it might make someone feel uncomfortable. This is not about being made to feel uneasy. This is about freedom, Miss Fitzgerald."

Clara was beginning to understand the motives behind the Sun Club. She still was not sure she completely agreed with it, but she was a person who was happy to let people live as they wished, as long as it didn't hurt anybody else. There were far worse things going on in the world, far nastier people, than someone who chose to sit on a beach without their clothes on.

They were now walking across the sand. She could see heads still bobbing out in the water.

"You mentioned you had seven guests in attendance," Clara remarked. "But I thought everyone had to attend in pairs."

"You are quite right that that is what our rules stipulate. Normally, we would completely enforce that rule, but one of our guests who wished to attend unfortunately could not bring his partner with him. She had been taken unwell, but he so wished to be here for the opening, and he agreed to be very conservative and discreet, so we allowed him to come. We would not normally make such an exception. But he is a person of great influence in the naturist world. And it did seem so cruel to make him wait till next year."

Clara was not sure what she felt about the fact that Miss Belle was already corrupting her own rules, bending them to suit her. It struck Clara that once you began down that route, it was a slippery slope.

"I can see you are concerned about this. Let me assure you that our seventh guest who goes by the name of Mr Hercules, has agreed not to mingle with any of the other guests while he is here. We have set aside specific times when he can use the beach and other places in complete privacy so that he is not breaking any rules when it comes to mingling with other people."

Clara was not going to query this. But she did pause when, after a moment, a thought came into her head.

"I count six heads in the ocean," she said to Miss Belle, "Which would be accurate considering what you've just told me. Where then, is your seventh guest? We have been around the whole house and gardens, and we have not seen anyone on their own."

Miss Belle came to a sharp stop herself. She suddenly seemed to realise the import of what Clara had said. She even counted the heads in the ocean just in case Clara had been mistaken.

Clara decided to state things bluntly. Just to press home the point.

"Miss Belle, you appear to be missing a guest."

Chapter Nine

M iss Belle was horrified by what Clara had said to her. The look of appal on her face made Clara almost regret what she had mentioned.

"Perhaps," she said. "Perhaps he has gone into town. Our guests are of course free to leave at any point as long as they do so clad, and he might have supposed that it would be a good time to do so when he couldn't use the beach."

"That is very possible," Clara agreed. "Your gatekeeper will of course know if he has left."

Miss Belle almost turned and ran all the way up the stairs and back across the lawn, but she paused before she did so. Clara felt something was wrong and saw the same feeling on her companion's face. It was like a strange tingling sensation running up and down the spine. Clara was not someone who believed in superstitions or premonitions. She was just used to trusting her instincts as a detective. Instincts, she told herself, were not based on anything fanciful. Instead, they were based upon experience, upon seeing patterns in behaviour.

Right now, her instincts were saying to her that the guest had not left the camp and that something may have happened. Miss Belle was clearly thinking the same.

"Maybe he's taken unwell," suggested Miss Belle. "I mean, it *is* cold today. Most of these people are very robust and hardy, but all of us can succumb at times to illness."

"Before we go rushing off to talk with your gatekeeper, we should instead have a look around the beach," Clara added. "Just in case he has become unwell and needs assistance."

"Yes, that is a good point," Miss Belle nodded. "There are some little coves along this stretch of private beach that a person could hide themselves away in."

They started to wander along the shoreline, leaving behind the guests who were still splashing about in the ocean and seemed quite content. Clara spotted the small little caves that Miss Belle was talking about. Miss Belle was saying how they owned more of the beach than they did the estate above; that they had several miles of it, in fact, and that there were signs on either end to indicate where their piece of the land began and finished.

"We cannot really fence it off," she told Clara as they walked. "But we do have signs to inform people that they're walking onto a nudist beach and that they should do so with the understanding of what they may see. The signs also state that it is private land. During the warmer months, when we are more popular, we are going to make sure that someone is around to patrol the area - possibly it will be Edward himself – just to make sure that no gawkers come to upset the guests, or worse, somebody who thinks they might try and cause harm to get us shut down."

Clara was only half listening to the woman, more interested in finding the missing guest. Miss Belle carried on talking and it was clearly a way to keep her nerves in check. Clara lost interest when she started to talk about the principles of naturism, how it had begun, and what it meant to them all. She was instead scanning the line of the cliffs, looking among the rocks, expecting at any moment to see something.

And then there it was; a glimpse of a pink foot which led up to a leg.

"I think someone is there," Clara pointed out what she had seen to Miss Belle.

They were still quite a distance away from the person. Miss Belle peered slightly shortsightedly ahead, and then started to hurry forward.

"Mr Hercules? Mr Hercules? Are you quite all right?"

"I assume Hercules is not his actual name?" Clara asked Miss Belle.

"We all have club names to mask our true identity. It is important to our guests because, of course, though they enjoy this, it could be a case that if someone else knew they came here, they would make problems for them or even damage their reputations."

The man who had gone under the name Hercules did not appear to be responding to their summonses. The way his leg remained perfectly still caused Clara to start to feel uneasy. She had seen enough corpses in her time to recognise when things were not quite right. Miss Belle, however, was hurrying fast ahead, still anticipating that Mr Hercules had taken unwell and needed some assistance.

Clara suddenly saw something on the sand that made her rush forward and grab Miss Belle's arm and hold her for a second.

"Let me go ahead," Clara told her.

"But..."

"I was a nurse in the war," Clara told her. "I've seen a lot of things, and I can certainly deal with any injuries or illness that Mr Hercules has succumbed to. Please just give me a moment to go ahead."

Miss Belle sensed something in Clara's tone that told her it was wiser if she stayed back, so she moved a pace away and allowed Clara to go on ahead alone.

What Clara had spotted was a patch of dark, rusty coloured sand. She was pretty certain it was blood stained and from the size of the patch that she could just glimpse, it didn't bode well for the unfortunate gentleman. She was thinking that perhaps Mr Hercules had slipped and fallen, cracking his head against the rocks of the cliff. Maybe, even worse, he had fallen down from the top; missed his footing, perhaps, or slipped on the grass, which she had noticed was damp. There were all manner of possible accidents he could have had happen to him while he was out here alone.

When she reached the rock that was masking the rest of his body from view, she did not pause for a second, but stepped around and looked down upon Mr Hercules. He was slumped back against the rocks. It looked a particularly uncomfortable pose, but she doubted he cared anymore, because aside from a nasty head wound, there were three deep gashes running across his chest.

She moved carefully around him, lifting up his hand that was resting beside him on the sand, and feeling for a pulse. As she expected, there was none. His face had already taken on a blueish tinge and there was a lot of blood around him. The gashes themselves did not look as though they would have resulted in death, though certainly they would have been an incapacitating injury. The head wound could easily have been fatal. The question was how he had come to be in this position with such injuries.

Clara had anticipated he would be completely naked, though his appearance did not shock her, since her mind was focusing instead on the fact that he was dead. She looked at his face to see if she recognised him.

Mr Hercules was a man in his thirties with dark, thick hair, a rather prominent nose, and a slight paunch to his belly. She was not sure if she would call him handsome. There was a narrowness to his chin which made his face look slightly sharp.

She did not recognise him. It was not someone from the town.

"What is happening?" Miss Belle called from behind the rock. "Does he need me to call for a doctor?"

Clara walked around the rock so that she could mask the view of the dead man for a little bit longer from Miss Belle. One never knew how someone would react to the sight of a dead body.

"Miss Belle, we're going to have to call the police, I'm afraid."

Miss Belle looked astonished. She clearly could not quite comprehend what Clara had said.

"The police?"

"I am sorry to say that something terrible has befallen, Mr Hercules. From the look of these injuries, he appears to have been deliberately attacked."

Miss Belle rushed forward. She refused to be stopped by Clara and jumped around the rocks to see for herself what she meant. She gasped at the sight of the fallen man.

"Poor Mr Hercules," she said, her voice quavering. "Who would do such a thing?"

She went a touch pale and pressed her fingers to her lips.

"I'm sorry, I feel quite unwell," she said and hastened away from the scene to compose herself.

Clara could do nothing for Mr Hercules, so she followed Miss Belle and placed a hand on her shoulder to console her.

"It is quite natural to be taken this way when you see a dead body," Clara told her. "Do not be ashamed about it."

"What were those gashes across his chest?" Miss Belle asked. "It looked like some animal had attacked him."

"I cannot say how they occurred. But I really think we need to call the police now, and I suggest we get your other guests back up to the house. Everyone will have to be questioned."

"Do you think someone did this because we are a nudist camp? They did it to try and shut us down?"

"It is rather a drastic way to end your naturist project," Clara said. "As unlikely as it would seem, I suppose we cannot dismiss any possibility."

"The publicity for all this will just be appalling," Miss Belle pressed her hands to either side of her head, her eyes wide.

She was in a state of shock, and Clara wanted to get her away from the beach as soon as possible.

"We must think practically, Miss Belle," she told her carefully. "We should now go back to the other guests and get them up to the house. Then we must call for the police. It is the only thing we can do."

"Yes, of course," Miss Belle was finally bringing herself back under control. "I am sorry. I don't know what came over me. It was irresponsible of me."

"Don't be so hard on yourself. It was a natural reaction. People don't go around seeing bodies like that all the time."

"You cannot believe how appalled I am to think I must summon the police," Miss Belle continued. "I know what they will be like. They will gawk and they will laugh, and they will make snide little comments. They are narrow-minded men."

"Inspector Park-Coombs isn't like that," Clara promised her. "I have a good working relationship with him. He will do everything he can to resolve this in a discreet and proper fashion."

Clara was briefly reminded of her dream that she had the night before and endeavoured not to shudder.

"Come now, we need to round up your guests."

Miss Belle nodded.

"Why don't you go ahead and use the telephone, while I try and explain it to everyone else?" she said.

Clara was agreeable to that. She had had enough of naked people for one day. She did not really want to see the remainder of the club members emerging from the ocean.

Leaving Miss Belle to sort out her guests, Clara headed for the steps and back up to the lawn. Her mind was whirling with possibilities. Why had this man been killed in such a savage manner?

She just hoped that Inspector Park-Coombs would be as understanding as she had suggested he would be.

Chapter Ten

It was several hours later when Clara managed to get home. Tommy, who had anticipated her being back much sooner than she was, was waiting for her, looking somewhat anxious about the delay. Clara was exhausted from her trip and did not want to immediately face his questions. But from the look on his face, she could see she was not going to get away without explaining the situation fully. The second he saw her, he noticed that something was amiss.

"What happened?" He asked urgently, heading forward, concerned about the paleness of his sister's face, the frown on her brow, and the way her mouth turned down at the corners. "You weren't propositioned by anybody, were you? Did they try something terrible?"

"Tommy, that is a ridiculous statement," Clara said. "I was not headed into some dragon's den where all the men were going to jump up on me at any second. It was all very proper. In fact, I only saw one naked person the entire time and they, unfortunately, happened to be dead."

This blunt statement had the effect she had hoped it would. Tommy fell silent and then backed away. "Did you say they were dead?"

"Yes. A tragedy has occurred at the Sun Club. Miss Belle was giving me a tour of the facilities. She intended, I think, to introduce me to her guests, when we discovered one of them was missing. We searched the beach and we found him. He had been killed."

"Murdered?" Tommy asked. "Are you absolutely certain it was not some accident?"

"No. He had three gashes across his chest. Park-Coombs said it looked like animal claws had slashed him. Though Dr Death has got to look at him properly to determine exactly what happened to him. There was a lot of blood. The poor man must have lain on the sand and bled out."

Tommy was now fully engaged in the matter and had completely forgotten about his earlier worries.

"You look like you need a cup of tea."

"I have had several while I was at the house explaining things to the inspector. No, what I need to do right now is sit down, take some weight off my feet. Poor Miss Belle was beside herself and she took a good deal of consoling before I could leave. She's upset enough about the fact that one of her guests has been murdered, but having the police buzzing around her house has really unsettled her. I promised her the police would be understanding, and certainly the inspector was, but I couldn't help noticing a few of the constables chuckling into their hands like schoolboys. They become so immature as soon as they wander into a place like that. I just hope they don't upset the guests. It would be a disaster for Miss Belle."

"Are you suggesting that you actually want the Sun Club to succeed?

Tommy looked appalled at even suggesting such a thing.

"I'm not saying that I want to become a member or anything like that, but they are doing nothing wrong, Tommy, and it seems to me Miss Belle was taking full responsibility for what was going on. She's put in place careful measures to protect people from anything sordid. Yes, I do have sympathy for her that something like this has happened so soon into her opening the club. It could end things before they've even begun."

Tommy motioned that they should head into the front parlour. He made sure his sister was settled down in her chair right before the fire, before he continued pressing her for information.

"You mentioned the marks on the man looked like animal claws?"

"That is the best way I can describe it," Clara said. "They were big. Bigger than a dog's. Three of them had gone from left to right in a downward motion across his chest."

"Like something had reared up and attacked him?" Tommy elaborated. "Something that could stand on its hind legs and use its front limbs like a human might."

"Where are you going with this?" Clara asked him.

Tommy got to his feet, holding up a finger to indicate she should just give him a moment. He fetched the newspaper and folded it back until he reached the small item of news that had been causing him worries all day after he had heard it from the man guarding the cattle. He pointed at it with a finger and gave her a moment to read it.

"A loose bear," Clara said, staring at the article with some surprise.

"Think about it, Clara. Bears stand up on their back legs to attack, and they use their paws differently to other animals. They would slash at someone in a horizontal fashion, whereas a big cat or dog would rear up and go in a vertical slashing motion."

Clara was not sure what to say about the article. The information within it was quite slim, but she had to admit that from what they had seen, it did seem to suggest that an animal had attacked Mr Hercules.

"What a terrible thing to happen," she said, reading the short snippet of news over and over as if somehow that would enable her to find out more information. "I suppose it is possible the bear wandered down to the beach looking for food and then it was disturbed by Mr Hercules."

"In a panic, it reared up and attacked him," Tommy suggested. "Bears have very bad vision and when they're spooked, they're notorious for going straight into an aggressive attack, whereas other animals would run away. There are often bear attacks in the United States and you hear about hikers being mauled by them."

"This is just dreadful," Clara said. "Though, in some ways, it would be a relief for Miss Belle. After all it's not her fault that a dangerous animal was roaming around the beaches. It could have attacked anyone. It just happened to come across Mr Hercules at her nudist camp. It would be considered the fault of the police for not finding the animal sooner, and the fault of the owner for not keeping it under better control."

"Then you are suggesting that this would be a better outcome for the Sun Club than if there was a murderer among them," Tommy nodded. "Which would make perfect sense."

"Do you suppose I ought to tell Inspector Park-Coombs what we've come across? Surely he'll work it out for himself once Dr Deáth has analysed the wounds more closely."

"I think we should stay out of it completely," Tommy said firmly. "It is not our case and not our problem. Interfering with the matters of the Sun Club could be tricky for us."

Clara gave her brother a stern look.

"You are nervous about our reputation. You are supposing that if we somehow became involved in the Sun Club, working for them on this matter, it would tarnish us."

"I was not going to go so far as to say something as dramatic as that," Tommy replied. "But if you want to put it that way, well, people are funny. It could mean we didn't get any more work from certain quarters."

"I take on any case," Clara told him firmly. "If someone needs help, I help them. In the past I have helped people who are criminals. How would this be any different, considering that everything that Miss Belle is doing is perfectly legal?"

Tommy saw that he was not going to win any argument on this subject, so he did not say anymore. He just hoped that the police would get this matter under control rapidly and that Miss Belle would not consider suggesting to Clara that she investigate the matter for her.

"It is rather worrying, however," Tommy continued, "to think that there could be this vicious animal walking around."

"Something has happened?"

They glanced up to see Annie was stood in the doorway and had overheard Tommy's last remark. "What has the bear done?"

The last thing Tommy wanted was for Annie to start worrying about bear attacks; it had been bad enough when she was considering that her chickens might be in danger. If she started to imagine that people would be at risk too, then they were going to suffer a lot of sleepless nights. Not to mention if she happened to tell the neighbours there could be pandemonium in the town before long. Of course, the odds were that it wouldn't be long before the newspapers got hold of this incident, and then everyone would know anyway. It was just the sort of story that the *Brighton Gazette* would be excited to run as it would increase sales for them and make a change from reporting on the local church fete.

"You mustn't get upset," Tommy told Annie.

His wife glared at him.

He was getting a lot of hard stares today.

"Tell me at once what is going on, Tommy," she said.

"A gentleman has been attacked, and has died," Clara was the one who replied. "He had gashes across his chest that suggest he had been attacked by a large animal."

Tommy had tried to give her a look, to tell her to shut up and say no more, but Clara was ignoring him. She decided it was better that Annie hear this information from them rather than to hear it from their neighbours. It was going to get out sooner rather than later. She knew from experience the police constables were prone to talking, especially when they had been on such an adventure as to a nudist club.

"The bear has killed someone?" Annie said in horror. "I knew we were all in danger!"

"We do not know it was the bear," Clara said firmly. "There was nothing in the snippet in the newspaper to indicate that the animal was dangerous."

"Clearly it is," Annie retorted. "Well, from now on we are not leaving the house, do you hear me? We cannot possibly go out anywhere. Not until that animal is caught."

"Annie!" Tommy groaned at her.

"I shall not hear any of it, Thomas Fitzgerald. You ought to remain indoors. Where it is safe."

"That is completely impractical," Clara told her gently. "Someone will have to go out for the shopping, at least, and the dogs need to be walked. Besides, I have cases to work on. Anyway, it's highly unlikely this bear will be found somewhere in town where there are so many people about."

"I don't like it, Clara," Annie snapped at her. "I'm going to be worried about you all the time."

"Then you will just have to worry," Clara sighed. "Bear or no bear, I am going to carry on with my work."

Chapter Eleven

N ews spreads fast, and bad news spreads even faster. Before the afternoon was done, the story of Mr Hercules' death was all over the town and the evening papers were stating that a murderous animal was on the loose.

It had to be stated that certain people in town did not seem to be entirely upset about the situation. Clara noted a few smirks among those of the prudish nature as they read the article. Some of her neighbours had already formed a committee which was going to oppose the Sun Club and this latest revelation seemed to add weight to their arguments. Clearly, running about nude was liable to get you attacked by wild animals, because it was a wild and feral way to behave. At least, that was the line they were taking.

Clara opted to ignore them. She was not convinced that this bear was roaming around simply to attack people. However, everyone had to admit that now there was a deep concern about what could be lurking outside in the shadows. Most people had been content in the knowledge that the bear would probably only appear at night, but the fact that someone had been attacked in the middle of the day, and on a stretch of the beach, which was not far from where a lot of people liked to walk, caused deep concern. Clara was not surprised that very quickly pamphlets were being pressed into hands, telling people to stay indoors. Reminding them to keep on their guard, to keep pets safely in the house and to run as fast as they could if they heard any sort of growling noise. She was not sure where these cheaply printed items came from. Someone clearly had their own little press, and they were enjoying creating pandemonium with the crudely published leaflets.

The police were slow to catch up. This did not surprise Clara either. She could imagine Inspector Park-Coombs' response to the situation would simply be a huff, and a twitch of his moustache. She doubted he took bears very seriously, and bear attacks even less seriously. But he could not ignore the chaos that was starting to run riot. Panic caught hold surprisingly quickly and when a group of worried people descended on the police station demanding to know what was being done to catch this bear, he was forced to act.

Clara happened to be present at that moment in time. She was giving her statement about the discovery of the unfortunate Mr Hercules, though she could not add much to what had already been said by Miss Belle.

Clara explained how she had not notice any footprints on the beach, either animal or human. Miss Belle confirmed that there had been quite a high tide that day, and it was entirely possible any footprints had been eradicated by the time they had found Mr Hercules.

"I can't see why a bear would be down on the beach in the first place," she added. "And it bothers me that no one appears to have heard Mr Hercules cry out, which surely he would have done if he had seen a bear about to attack him. The swimmers were not that far away."

"He might have been caught unawares," Park-Coombs responded calmly.

"That is, of course, a possibility."

"Whatever truly happened, we have a situation on our hands that is unravelling rapidly. A bear on the loose and people baying for its blood," Park-Coombs rumbled.

"What are you going to do to try and calm down the situation?" Clara asked him.

"Everything I can," Park-Coombs answered. "My constables are going to make extra patrols around the perimeters of the town to try and spot the creature. I have already sent a notice to the Chief Constable, suggesting we call in an expert on the subject of bears."

"An expert?" Clara said, frowning.

"I was thinking along the lines of maybe a zookeeper, or one of those people who go on safaris. Someone who understands animals and can find them. After all, bears are not common creatures around here and the average local Squire can't compare hunting foxes to hunting one of these. We need someone who can track it and capture it."

It had been at that point in the conversation they were distracted by the arrival of a flustered looking constable, who said there was a gaggle of people in the foyer demanding to see the inspector. He explained how a number of them were women over a certain age, who were waving umbrellas and demanding to know what the police were going to do to keep them safe.

There was nothing worse than a mob of angry middle-aged women descending on the police station and the constable, who was barely a boy himself, looked utterly out of his depth.

"I better go deal with this," Park-Coombs groaned. "It never rains, but it pours."

He rose and showed Clara out of his office. From the upstairs landing, they could see the gaggle of people in the foyer. They did seem to mainly compose of older women, and they all looked very agitated and furious. Some were screaming that their children would be eaten in their beds.

Clara wisely exited out of the back door of the police station, nodding to some of the police constables as she went by. Out in the street again, she could think at last.

She knew this was none of her business, she had not been asked to investigate the death of Mr Hercules. She also knew she was being irresistibly drawn to poking her nose into the matter. She never could refuse a mystery.

"Concentrate on the matter at hand," Clara told herself firmly, then she pulled a face.

Concentrating on the matter in hand meant dealing with Mrs Wilton and trying to convince her they could do nothing about the Sun Club.

Clara would have preferred to be dealing with an irate bear.

Chapter Twelve

Mrs Wilton was disgruntled that it was early evening before Clara turned up on her doorstep. Mrs Wilton generally was not one to snap at people, she just became more and more flustered. But on this occasion it was plain to see she was angry, and that anger was directed at Clara.

"How dare you wait this long to tell me what is going on?" Mrs Wilton said to Clara the second she opened the door and saw her there.

Mrs Wilton was going through one of those periods of time when she was lacking a maid. She went through maids at a surprisingly swift rate.

Clara had no excuse to offer her, so she merely stated the truth.

"I have been very busy, Mrs Wilton, with the situation at the Sun Club. I had to go and give a statement to the police, and it took all day to get things sorted."

Mrs Wilton huffed. Not impressed by this excuse.

"I heard about it all just after luncheon. Surely you could have got here sooner?"

"I can assure you I could not," Clara persisted.

She was not going to apologise for the fact that she had been doing her duty.

"I would have thought you would have come at once. My son could be in danger."

"I don't believe that the situation at the Sun Club is in itself inherently dangerous," Clara explained. "While the bear attack certainly occurred there, that does not mean that it was linked to the club. It could have happened anywhere. Your son is in no more danger there than if he was strolling along the cliffs."

This information was meant to calm Mrs Wilton. Instead, it caused her to go a strange colour of violet and look increasingly alarmed. Mrs Wilton's son had vanished shortly after the war, and she had thought she had lost him. She had never truly recovered from the trauma and shock of those terrible months, and when he returned to her she had become exceptionally clingy, worried that the second he went out of her sight, he might disappear again. Clara's statement had not helped that concern.

"He went for a walk on the cliffs just now," Mrs Wilton said, peering out of the door.

She had not so far invited Clara in, another sign of how annoyed she was with her.

"It was just a figure of speech," Clara promised. "I don't believe anyone else is in danger from the bear."

"But that's just it. How can you state that? That man at the Sun Club clearly didn't think he was in danger, else he wouldn't have been going around without any clothes on," Mrs Wilton shuddered at the thought of the man being attacked naked.

Somehow that made it worse. She found that she was mentally envisioning items of the male anatomy that she really ought not to envision when she pictured the scene.

"Can I come in, Mrs Wilton, and we can have a proper conversation," Clara suggested.

Mrs Wilton was still reluctant. She looked as though she was going to keep Clara on the doorstep as part of a penance for not coming sooner to speak to her. Ultimately, she agreed that Clara should come in. She showed her through to the front room and they sat together, though there was no tea to accompany their discussion.

"Was it very nasty?" Mrs Wilton asked.

"Well, there was a lot of blood," Clara shrugged. "I don't think that Mr Hercules suffered in any way. It looked to me like he fell quite quickly, and I think he banged his head as he went down. I don't suppose he knew much about it after that. It's even possible that the bear did not attack him until after he was already dead."

"Why would it do something like that?" Mrs Wilton asked in horror.

"Bears are scavengers, primarily," Clara replied. "They can hunt, but they are better at cleaning up after other animals. That is why they encroach on towns. They scavenge through rubbish bins. It's possible that the bear simply stumbled across Mr Hercules and was curious enough to investigate, and then a noise or some other thing caused it to run off."

"You're trying to make me feel better, but you are not," Mrs Wilton shook her head. "I have talked to Edward and told him he is not to return to that Sun Club, not while this bear is on the loose and if I have my way about it, there won't be a Sun Club after that."

"As far as I can see, Mrs Wilton, there is nothing occurring at the club that is either illegal or immoral."

"How can you even say that Clara, when they walk around with no clothes on?"

"But nudity is not a crime," Clara pointed out. "At least, not when it's done in private. The human body, in itself, is not immoral. I suppose it is more a case of what people do with it."

"Clara, you're starting to sound a little bit too liberal for my liking."

"What I am trying to explain, Mrs Wilton, is that I don't think there's anything much you can do about the Sun Club. They're not breaking any rules. They have permits to be here and from what I saw of the estate, they're taking great steps to ensure that nobody who isn't a guest can see people without their clothes on. They're not going to become a public hazard or public nuisance. If anything, they value their privacy."

"There will be orgies and other such debauchery going on," Mrs Wilton said in alarm, her voice raising an octave.

Clara now saw what was on her mind. She was thinking it was some sort of love club where people came together for a bit of hanky panky.

"It is not a brothel, Mrs Wilton. The people have to attend as couples, and they can't switch around with each other. There are rules in place."

"Of course, they *tell* you there are rules. That is how they lure you in, how they make you think they're all innocent and friendly. But before you know it, it all comes out. There will be ladies getting pregnant by men they barely know and other such affairs."

Mrs Wilton was not going to be convinced by any argument that Clara could offer.

"I'm sorry, Mrs Wilton, but from a legal point of view, I can't offer you anything. I didn't see anything at the club that could be deemed illegal. That was what you wanted me to look for, to find something that they were doing they shouldn't be doing."

"I know you tried, Clara," Mrs Wilton nodded. "Though I suspect you were far too ready to listen to the proprietor's lies. You're far too generous on that front, too open-minded. Sometimes one has to see things from a different perspective."

Clara did not suggest that the perspective she was referring to sounded like one that was stifled, old fashioned and somewhat irrational. She knew it wasn't going to achieve anything, and she still hadn't summed up the courage to tell Mrs Wilton that her son Edward was heavily involved with the Sun Club as one of its founders.

"I just want Edward to leave it well alone," Mrs Wilton folded her arms and hugged herself.

She looked suddenly distressed, and Clara saw a glimmer of something else. Maybe it wasn't just about the Sun Club and the fact that people went around nude. Maybe it was the fact that Edward was drifting away from his mother. That he was branching out, as all young men should, and building a life for himself away from her. After the war, he had come home because his mother was in such a bad way, both emotionally and financially. He had stayed at home to help her get set up properly. He'd made sure she was financially secure again and he provided a great deal of comfort to her. But now several years had passed, and it was time he thought about himself. His mother could survive without him, at least from a practical point of view. Clara sensed that Mrs Wilton was not keen on having an empty house once more, or of being alone. It was something she feared worse than death itself.

"I'm sorry I could not be of any more use," Clara told her.

"You tried, Clara. I understand. No matter. I have joined one of these groups that is protesting the Sun Club. We're going to petition the County Council to have them evicted. There must be something we can do about public morality."

"As I didn't do very much at all," Clara continued. "I don't see any reason I should charge you for what I've done already."

Mrs Wilton shook her head.

"I always pay you for your services, no matter how small they are."

"I really don't feel I warrant being paid for what I did today," Clara replied. "I just asked a few questions. Can we just agree that it was a favour done for a friend?"

"I would much prefer to pay you for your time. It is only fair, you worked hard."

Mrs Wilton refused to be persuaded and Clara eventually gave in. Mrs Wilton considered it a matter of pride to be able to pay Clara, considering that on the first case she had hired her for, she had been unable to pay up her dues immediately. She headed off into another room to fetch her chequebook. While she was gone, the front door opened and closed. Edward wandered into the front room.

Clara had not seen him in a couple of years. He had grown into a tall, good looking young man, slightly slender in the face and with high temples where his hair was starting to recede but still dashing. The small moustache he had grown on his upper lip made him look somewhat debonair.

"Hello, Miss Fitzgerald."

"Hello, Mr Wilton," Clara nodded at him.

She didn't know if his mother had told him what she had hired Clara for this time. She didn't want to start explaining herself.

"I was actually thinking of coming and seeing you," Edward said, wandering into the room and standing near Clara.

She was surprised at this statement.

"Oh," she said, wondering if he was about to criticise her for going to the Sun Club and digging around in his private affairs.

"Yes. I had a word with Miss Belle. You've met Daisy?"

Clara did not reply, though she felt a slight reddening in her cheeks. She did not often blush, but she on this occasion she felt as though she'd been caught out digging around behind Edward's back in a rather unseemly fashion.

"I know my mother asked you to go to the Sun Club," Edward

explained. "She told me she was going to do it. I also know you were very kind to Daisy, and she found you very genuine. She said you took care of her when you found Mr Hercules."

"I just did what anyone would do," she told him. "It doesn't take much in this life to be kind to someone."

"Yet so many would not bother to make the effort. Look, could we have a chat?"

He stopped speaking abruptly as his mother re-entered the room.

"Ah, Edward, you are home."

"Evening, Mother. I'm going to walk Miss Fitzgerald back to her house. I don't think it's right, under the current circumstances, that she should go home alone. I won't be long and then I'll be back in time for supper."

He didn't give his mother time to argue, not that she could criticise his act of chivalry. She barely had a chance to hand over the cheque to Clara before Edward was whisking her out of the door under the pretence that he needed to get her home before it got too late.

Chapter Thirteen

"I am deeply worried about the impact this could have on Daisy and the Sun Club," Edward explained as they started to walk through the dark back to Clara's home. She didn't actually need anyone to walk her home. She was quite capable of taking care of herself. She had a torch and in an emergency, she knew all sorts of ways to keep herself safe.

"It was an unfortunate accident," Clara replied. "No one could have known that a bear would come along."

"It was an unfortunate accident that happened to happen at the Sun Club," Edward elaborated. "My point is, it's going to create a scandal. Already there are people outside the gates demanding that we close, as if the bear was somehow an act of God designed to prove how scandalously we are behaving."

"Surely people have not gone so far as that?" Clara said, wondering who was stirring up such trouble.

"I am only stating exactly what has been stated to me," Edward continued. "And yes, they have gone as far as to say that. There is one particular vicar who stands outside the gates with a placard claiming that we were all the devil's children and that everything happening to us is well deserved for immoral behaviour."

"Well, that is not very nice at all," Clara huffed. "It does not say much for this vicar."

"No, and it could be the end of the Sun Club before it even begins. If this gets out among the nudist community, they won't want to come to us, not because of the bear attack, which no one could have foreseen, but because of all the hatred and antagonism that will be going around locally. No one wants to go to a place where they think people might throw eggs at them or call them whores."

He had a fair point, but Clara was not sure how she could help him in that regard.

"The loss of Mr Hercules is perhaps the worst thing that could have happened," Edward spoke fast as they walked. "You know who he is in reality, don't you? Or rather, who he was."

"I'm afraid I don't. I didn't recognise him."

"Mr Hercules is the son of a very notable politician. One who has a lot to say about public morality and the scandalous behaviour of the youth of today. He would be quick enough to penalise us all for what has happened."

"It does sound a very bad situation," Clara agreed with him. "Certainly not the sort of thing that is going to help a business start off on the right foot."

"I knew you would understand, Clara. You have your head screwed on right. I said to Daisy, 'Clara Fitzgerald will be the one to sort this for us.'"

Clara was not sure she liked this statement. She was slightly concerned about what it meant.

"Sort this?" She asked uneasily.

"Exactly. We need you to look into this matter. I mean, the police will do a good job, but they will only see what is before their eyes and, as we have already discovered, they cannot be trusted to keep their mouths shut."

Clara had her own suspicions that it was a gossiping constable who had tipped off the *Brighton Gazette*.

"I can tell you now that a lot of our guests won't be inclined to speak to the police. They simply won't feel safe revealing who they really are or speaking freely to them. It will stifle the investigation."

"Then you must speak to them and explain the necessity of cooperating with the police."

"They're not the sort of people who you speak to like that," Edward smiled at her. "They're the sort of people with a lot of money who do things exactly as they choose to. And dare I say, some of them don't hold the police in very high regard."

Clara could imagine that; though she had not met the other guests she was under the impression they were from the upper classes, the ones with money, the ones who didn't care much for the police and would not be inclined to speak openly with Inspector Park-Coombs. She could already picture how badly things would go for him when he tried to interview them, and how annoyed he would end up. When he was annoyed, Park-Coombs lost his temper and said things that were not wise. That would only make things worse.

"Look, couldn't I just hire you to investigate this all for us?" Edward asked. "You're not working for my mother anymore, are you? Therefore, it won't be a conflict of interest."

Clara thought of the cheques she had just popped away into her handbag.

"Well, no, I'm not working for her. I didn't really succeed in what she wanted me to achieve, and I think she has decided that I am not the right person to dig up scandal on the Sun Club. I am too liberal, apparently."

Edward chuckled heartily.

"That is my mother's favourite derogatory comment at the moment," he said. "She uses it against me all the time."

They walked on for a few steps without saying anything. Then Clara glanced up at him.

"What caused you to be involved with the Sun Club in the first place?"

"Oh, well, that is very easy. It was a woman," Edward smiled at her. "To be precise, it was Daisy. I was down in London for a bit visiting some cousins and I met her at a social event. We got talking and we found that we had a lot in common. For the remainder of my time in London, we spent as many hours together as we could, finding various excuses to be together. Somewhere along the line we started talking about the naturist movement. Daisy was very interested in the whole thing, saying how healthy it was, how freeing, and she convinced me."

"It is one thing to share a passion, another thing to start a business together, especially when it is something that is so new and radical."

"True," Edward nodded. "But it made sense. I had been looking for something to do with my time, something I could invest in and really make a go of. I have the income to spare. I've made sure my mother's financial investments are functioning profitably, and I have my own money. I just wanted something more. I didn't want to just sit around being employed by someone else.

"The more we talked about it, the more I liked the idea of running this Sun Club. I think the turning point was when Daisy and I travelled to another nudist camp to investigate the situation. It was actually someone's home where they invited their friends to come and experience the naturist culture. It was very liberating.."

Clara was still uncomfortable imagining people going around completely naked in the company of others. Walking beside Edward, she found herself starting to picture him without his clothes on. The thought ran though her mind before she could stop it.

"So, you decided to set up in Brighton," she said, aiming to distract herself with practical thoughts.

"It seemed a logical thing, what with the waters being health-giving and this already being a tourist spot. Then I spied the house on the cliffs, and it was up for sale, and I told Daisy about it. She has more money than I. She inherited it recently. As soon as she heard about it, she was all for the idea and bought the place outright. I've invested a little of my own money, but mostly it's my time that's going into the thing. I'm the one in charge of booking visitors and making sure the place is maintained, watching over the staff, that sort of thing. It is very important to both of us that this succeeds Clara. It's not just about the ideology and wanting to stand up to the people who are so narrow minded here. It's also the fact that we have both invested a lot of money in this. We would be quite poor without it."

The bleak look that came on to Edward's face told Clara this was completely true. He had put a lot of himself and a lot of his own money into the Sun Club and he could not afford for it to fail before it had begun.

"Seeing as I don't have anything else happening at the moment, and I'm not working for your mother anymore, I suppose it would be perfectly all right for me to help you," Clara finally said.

He looked delighted at this information and the smile returned to his face.

"You cannot know how relieved I feel hearing you say that."

"I can imagine," Clara nodded.

"Will you begin at once? We cannot spare any time."

"Of course," Clara said. "However, I must repeat that I believe the matter appears to have been purely an accident. A very unfortunate incident with this local escaped bear."

"But it would be good to have an outside person looking into things and to be absolutely sure," Edward was enthusiastic. "The way the inspector talked to us, he made it seem as though there was a possibility of something more sinister having occurred."

"That is just the way that Inspector Park-Coombs' mind works," Clara promised him. "I will look into it further and find out exactly what happened to Mr Hercules. Though it would be helpful if I could begin by knowing his actual name."

"Well, since the police know it, and he's deceased, I don't see why you shouldn't," Edward nodded. "His name was O'Brien. Gerald O'Brien. You might have heard of his father, Haitham O'Brien."

Clara was not entirely familiar with politics. They were something that tended to happen on the periphery of her attention. But she did have an inkling she knew the name.

"He is the epitome of conservative," Edward continued. "I doubt he knew of his son's inclinations. He could be just as much a threat to us as any of the little protest groups starting up in town. He could shut us down, Clara."

"I will do everything I can, Edward."

Edward was glad to hear this, and he held out his hand for her to shake on the matter. She appreciated the gesture.

They were at her house, and he opened the garden gate for her.

"I will let Daisy know that you are coming."

"May I suggest that at some point you have a discussion with your mother about exactly how you are involved with the Sun Club," Clara added before he departed.

"I don't think she will take it well, Clara."

"You can't keep it from her forever. At some point you're going to have to explain to her what you are doing."

"Maybe. Or maybe it'll simply never come up. She's never been particularly interested in my work."

Clara thought that was a rather hopeless plan, but what else could she say to him? She wished him goodnight, and headed inside to start making her own plans on how she was going to help the Sun Club.

Chapter Fourteen

T he following day, Tommy went out for a walk with the dogs as usual. While he had his eyes peeled for any sign of something large and brown, he had decided that he wasn't going to live his life hiding away in the house. After all, he had gone through nearly all the war, having avoid being killed. Why should he suddenly start to hideaway in the house because of one solitary bear? There could be dangers any day of the week outside. There could be open manholes that you fell down, or runaway carriages that could take you out. You could be involved in a bus accident. Just because the bear was a known danger did not change anything.

He had not been walking for very long on the local common when he was hailed by another young man he knew who also walked his dogs there most days. He didn't actually know the young man's name, though he knew that his dog, a large Irish wolfhound, was called Paddy. Paddy sauntered over and touched noses with Pip, who was always glad to see a playmate. Bramble gave a small growl and headed behind Tommy, refusing to come out again while the bigger dog was hanging around.

While Pip and Paddy went for run around the common, Paddy's owner wandered over to talk to Tommy.

"Have you seen the newspaper today?" He asked.

Tommy had not yet got around to buying the morning edition.

"I have not," he admitted.

"There was a big advertisement in it. Someone with a lot of money is asking for people to come and have a go at catching the bear. There is a reward of fifty pounds."

"That is a lot of money," Tommy agreed. "Does it say who has put up the money?"

"Not specifically. You have to reply to the newspaper office for the reward with proof that you've killed the bear."

"Killed it," Tommy said in alarm.

"Well, yes. How else are you going to capture it?"

"I thought the owner of the bear would like it back alive and well?"

"Well, he has not posted a fifty-pound reward," the young man continued. "In any case, with all that's gone on, it can't be allowed to keep roaming around. It killed a man after all."

"It might have just been defending itself," Tommy said.

"You can't have monsters like that on the loose. Might kill a child next."

"I very much doubt it's going to attack a child," Tommy said firmly.

"Well, a dog, then?" The young man pointed at Bramble, who was still hunkering down behind Tommy. "Yours would be but a mouthful for it. Imagine how you would feel then."

Tommy glanced down at the small poodle.

"I would be devastated," Tommy agreed. "But it's not as though the animal would do it maliciously, it would just do it because it was a bear."

"Whatever we think of the matter, the reward is out there, and you mark my words, by this afternoon you'll see a dozen people in the town hoping to claim it. News like that spreads fast. It'll probably be in the national papers before tomorrow."

Tommy dreaded to think of the chaos that would cause. The thought of all those hunters, both skilled and unskilled, coming down to try their luck at catching the bear made him shudder to think of it. You never knew if an inexperienced hunter might mistake a bouncy Labrador for a bear.

"Of course, I'm not particularly worried about Paddy," the young man continued. "Irish wolfhounds were built for hunting big creatures, hence the name. He could take on a bear, I reckon."

The young man looked proudly at his large dog, who was currently rolled on his back, while Pip jumped over him repeatedly and ragged at his ears.

"I rather hope neither of us have to worry about that," Tommy said. "With any luck, the animal will be spotted and captured alive sooner rather than later."

"You are optimistic. It's not as though the authorities are taking any interest in the matter," the young man snorted. "They've made no effort whatsoever to try and catch it. I mean, there must be people they can call upon to do something. No wonder someone has decided they need to offer a reward."

Tommy was mulling this all over as he headed home after the walk. He didn't like to think of the unfortunate bear being hunted down and shot. He also was slightly concerned about how many other creatures might accidentally find themselves in front of the hunters' guns in their enthusiasm to catch the bear.

He found Clara in the parlour, working on a few notes before she headed out that day.

"Apparently there is a reward being offered for the capture of the bear," he told her grimly as he stepped into the room. "Dead, of course."

"That's sad," Clara replied. "Though it's out of our hands, I suppose. We need to go back to the Sun Club today. Try and find out a bit more about Mr Hercules or should I now say Gerald O'Brien?"

"That certainly brings a new aspect to the case," Tommy agreed. "You do know about his father, I suppose."

"Edward made some vague mention of him. He's rather conservative."

"He's rather a lot of things. He has been quoted as saying that he doesn't think the poor should be helped because they've put themselves into that position by breeding too much."

"Charming," Clara scowled. "So, he doesn't appreciate that a lack of education opportunities is also playing a part in their circumstance?"

"No, he is one of these people who think any person can pull themselves up by their bootstraps, just because one or two fellows have done so. He was all for the clearing out some slums in London, but unfortunately he was not inclined to agree that something had to be done to rehouse the poor people they were going to remove from the area. In fact, I do believe he was quoted by one paper as saying that they might as well stay in their houses while they were pulled down and that would solve the problem."

"He sounds positively delightful," Clara sighed.

"I presume his son, Gerald, was a very different kettle of fish," Tommy shrugged. "After all, he was inclined to go to the Sun Club."

"Either that or he just liked to protest and upset his father. People do things like that to offend a parental figure who is particularly adamant in their views."

"Maybe. Still, it is very sad what happened to him. I don't see how we can do much more than confirm that a bear attacked him."

"Rattling out the truth will make a big difference. Having it all laid out properly and plainly will take away these rumours. I think that's really what Edward is looking for. Maybe he's also hoping that I can somehow convince these protesters that his Sun Club is not a haven for immorality, but I think that might be pushing our luck."

"Our first stop is going to be the morgue and Dr Deáth?"

"That seems a logical place to start. Might as well find out exactly what killed Mr Hercules, or shall I say Gerald."

"I wonder why he chose that name," Tommy mused.

"Hercules was a hero. He was mighty and powerful."

"Yes, but he was also a murderer. He killed his own family. That's why he had to do his twelve labours. It was his penance. Many of the stories about him don't paint him in a particularly good light."

"Even so, he was still considered a hero, and most people don't delve that deeply into his legend."

"True," Tommy nodded. "I was just wondering if there was anything more to the identification than purely the obvious. Hercules didn't get on with his father."

"He was fathered by Zeus, wasn't he?"

"Yes, and he didn't get on with him or have much to do with him. But he also didn't have a good relationship with his foster father. The husband of his mother who was cuckolded by the Olympian god."

"It could be said that Hercules stood for all young men who cannot stand their fathers and wish to be better than them," Clara supposed.

It was a clever way of looking at things and Tommy liked it.

"Possibly we're giving Gerald too much credit for being that clever," he said.

"Let's get over to the morgue and find out what happened to him,"

Clara rose. "On the way, we better keep our eyes open for any bear hunters who think they might be clever enough to come here and solve our problem for us."

Tommy pulled a face.

"Poor bear," he said.

Clara patted his shoulder lightly.

"Poor bear," she agreed.

Chapter Fifteen

D r Deáth had been the coroner for the police for several years
now. He liked his job. It was an awkward thing to say, but he
did. It wasn't that he liked seeing people dead or those who had been
brutally murdered, but he did like finding out what had happened
to them and giving their families some degree of peace. He was a
small man who was always humming to himself as he went about his
morgue. He dressed neatly, if slightly old fashioned, and was getting
quite portly in his later years. When he was not tending to the dead, he
liked bridge parties and the opera. There was quite often music playing
on a gramophone as he conducted his autopsies. For the most part,
he was always there alone. He did have an assistant who came in for a
few hours each day. But there was not a great call for his services most
of the time. Dr Deáth ran the place by himself and was quite content
with that.

He was, however, always glad to see visitors, especially Clara and
Tommy, as he knew he was going to get a good conversation from
them. He greeted them warmly as they came in. Just a couple of
months ago, they had helped him with his own difficult dilemma,
a situation that had arisen due to a wager he had placed among his
friends. The matter had given him an unhappy insight into a few

aspects of his personal character he had not previously understood, and he had been slightly chagrined at what had been revealed. He still felt a tad embarrassed that Clara had happened to see that there was a slightly darker side to him, though, compared to a lot of people, Dr Deáth's dark side was really quite mundane.

He had not seen the detectives since that case and was glad to welcome them now, even though he knew they were there on business.

"You will be here about the bear case," he said in a jolly voice. "If you go down to the woods today, you better go in disguise."

"I am not sure that little ditty is in good taste today," Clara told him, though she smiled to soften the criticism.

"I cannot help myself. I keep thinking about it the whole time I am working. I never supposed I would be in a situation where I would be dealing with a bear attack."

"It is slightly unusual in England," Clara agreed. "We came along just to see if you could tell us more about what happened to Mr O'Brien."

Dr Deáth motioned to a covered table just behind him. On it, the shapes and dips beneath the blanket indicated that there was a body. This was a quite familiar sight when they entered the morgue and neither Clara nor Tommy ever reacted these days to seeing a corpse lying about. In some regards they had become quite immune to the sight of the dead. Tommy reflected that it almost was somewhat disturbing at how blasé they had become about the situation.

"What do you want to know about the fellow?" Dr Deáth asked. "I've done a full postmortem."

"Suppose we begin with how he died? Was it the bear that killed him?"

"It was blood loss," Dr Deáth told her. "The fancy term is exsanguination. However, I cannot tell you for certain if the bear attack alone was responsible for his death."

"Now you have my interest," Clara said, coming closer. Tommy was just a step behind her, also interested in what was occurring.

Dr Deáth walked over to the table which contained the body and folded back the sheet. The young man's head had been shaved and there was a line around the top of the scalp, where the skin had been pulled back so that Dr Deáth could get to his brain.

"He had a nasty head wound on the back of his head," Dr Deáth elaborated. "And that had bled quite a lot. Also, it had fractured the skull and there was a shard of bone close to penetrating the brain. I don't think it had done any damage, but it was certainly nasty enough to have the potential to do so. The head wound could have caused the blood loss, as could the scratches that were across his chest. Either of them could have caused him to bleed out, or, for that matter, both of them together."

"Which came first, though?" Clara asked. "The head wound or the scratches on his chest?"

"I'm afraid that is rather difficult to determine," Dr Deáth shrugged. "It could be that he was slashed by the bear and fell back and hit his head. There were certainly plenty of rocks around the scene and one of them was caked with his blood. On the other hand, he could have fallen first and knocked his head, and then the bear came along later. Drawn in by the scent of his blood. Though, in that regard, I would have expected to have found bite marks rather than claw slashes."

Tommy was peering down at Gerald O'Brien's skull. He was trying not to dwell too much on what Dr Deáth was explaining so calmly.

"It doesn't tell us a great deal at all," Clara sighed.

"Were you expecting me to prove he had been murdered?" Dr Deáth asked her, knowing that this tended to be Clara's territory.

"I had considered the possibility," Clara explained. "There's been quite a lot of trouble around the Sun Club, though realistically the odds were the young man had just suffered a misfortune. What else can you tell me about him?"

"Nothing particularly insightful," Dr Deáth shrugged. "He was in good health, though if he'd been alive, I would have suggested he cut down on his smoking habits. I cannot comment on his desire to go around naked. It doesn't seem to have either impaired his health or improved it."

"I suppose that is something," Tommy remarked. "What about the slash marks themselves? Is it definite they came from the claws of a bear?"

"Honestly, I have nothing to compare them to," Dr Deáth explained. "What I can tell you is that they were made by the incision of a sharp object slashed in a diagonal motion. Whatever the objects were, there happened to be four of them, which would be consistent with the claws of a bear. However, I have never had to examine claw marks before in this regard, and so I cannot say for certain that it would be a bear's claws that did this. Though in truth, I have no reason to suppose they are anything else."

"I suppose the bear came along and started prodding around at the body looking for a meal?"

"Or it knocked him down when it slashed him, and he hit his head. Possibly it then ran off in a panic. Not because it had killed him, of course, but because of the commotion that had been caused. It may even be the bear was running off as he fell. Bears are most likely to attack when in a defensive mood. At least that is what I've read, and of course, it's the wrong time of year for them to be protecting their young."

"And it's not as though we live in North America," Clara pointed out. "Where bears are a slightly bigger problem than they are here."

"Have you seen they've put out a reward for this capture of this bear?" Dr Deáth added.

"I have, and I'm slightly disappointed that such extremes have been resorted to. But then again, I'm also disappointed that the original owner of the animal has not done more to claim it and resolve the situation. Not that I particularly think it is a great danger to people as long as they are sensible. But it could deal harm to farm animals when it gets hungry."

"You are saying that when you have a man with claw marks across his chest lying before you," Dr Deáth pointed out.

"Yes, but we have no idea exactly what happened. He might have tried to scare the animal off and that resulted in this attack. In general, wild animals don't go out of their way to savage people unless they are rabid. They tend to be more scared of us than we are of them."

"Oh, but I've heard the stories from India and so forth about man eating tigers. The ones that got a taste for eating people."

"Those stories are particularly rare," Clara shook her head. "And how many of them are true is another matter. They make for a good tale after all."

"You are such a spoilsport, Clara," Dr Deáth chuckled. "In any case, it's not as though I am going to go out hunting a bear. It is not the sort of thing I agree with. Though I do know a couple of my friends have already decided to give it a shot."

"That is what worries me more," Tommy remarked. "The thought of all these amateur hunters wandering around, shooting at anything that looks about the shape and size of a bear. I think you're going to see more accidents occurring before you know it."

Dr Deáth was inclined to agree with him. Anytime there was a lot of men wandering around with guns, there was always a chance of someone getting hurt by accident.

"I keep meaning to have a word with Inspector Park-Coombs about it, suggesting he clamps down on the matter. Of course, it's a free country and you can't really tell people to not go around with the old hunting rifle since they're legal."

"Let's just hope the bear has had the sense to leave the county," Tommy shrugged.

"You are disappointed," Dr Deáth said to Clara, noticing her expression. "You wanted me to tell you something different."

"It is not so much disappointment as not knowing how to proceed with this. I have been asked to try and find the truth about what happened to Gerald O'Brien for the benefit of the Sun Club. They're concerned how much scandal this is going to cause for them. But as far as I can see, the truth is that he was the unfortunate victim of an escaped bear, and I can't change that."

"Sorry," Dr Deáth said solemnly. "It's just impossible for me to tell you what happened first, the head wound or the slash marks. I can tell you he was alive when both of them occurred. But not the sequence. There was too much blood all over the scene for me to be able to determine which came first."

"We completely understand," Tommy assured him. "It was just one of those vague hopes we had."

"If I can think of anything else, I'll let you know," Dr Deáth promised them.

They thanked him and headed on their way. Once outside, Tommy turned to Clara.

"Is there really any point carrying on with this case when the truth is laid out before us already? Surely we're just wasting the time of Edward and Daisy. Not to mention our own time and effort."

Clara was inclined to agree with him, but something was nagging at the back of her mind.

"I don't know, Tommy. Maybe we are wasting our time. But I also wonder if there is something else here that I am missing. Mr Hercules came to the club all on his own, which is against the rules. Now I know the bending of their own rules is entirely up to them. But could it be that there was something more behind the reason he came alone than what we know?"

"Now you are trying to make a mystery out of nothing," Tommy told her plainly. "Leave it alone, Clara. The young man had an unfortunate accident. That's all that we can say about it."

"I suppose you are right," Clara agreed. "We should perhaps go to Edward and Daisy right away and tell them that there's no more we can do. To keep digging around would just be wasting their money."

"I think that sounds like a very good idea," Tommy nodded. "Sometimes there just isn't a mystery to solve."

Chapter Sixteen

T hey headed immediately back to the Sun Club, deciding it was best to speak to Daisy and Edward at once. They were welcomed gladly by Daisy, though Edward was not present. She showed them into her front room, which overlooked the main lawns. There was no sign of the guests, which was somewhat of a relief to Tommy.

"What do you have to tell me?" Daisy asked. "I know Edward has been speaking to you on this matter. We are very concerned about the implications this could have for the continuation of the Sun Club."

"We have spoken to the coroner," Clara explained. "To all intents and purposes, it looks as though the unfortunate Mr O'Brien suffered a tragic accident. It is difficult to say whether the slashes on his chest were made before or after he hit his head, either way there was no indication of anything malicious happening."

"He hit his head?" Daisy said, trying to keep up with what Clara had just said.

"Yes, there were signs of an injury to the back of Mr O'Brien's head. He bled to death."

"There was certainly a lot of blood around him," Daisy agreed. "I did not know you could bleed to death from a bang to the head though."

"You can bleed to death from any wound if it's serious enough," Tommy explained. "He fractured his skull as well when he fell back onto a sharp rock. Dr Deáth does not think that caused fatal damage, but it certainly would have impaired his ability to move and probably knocked him unconscious. Coupled with the slashes across his chest there was nothing he could do to prevent himself from bleeding out."

They had been rather blunt in their statements, as Clara tended to be when she was explaining something to a client. Daisy now looked troubled and pale. She sat down sharply on the nearest chair and placed a hand to her temple.

"This is terrible," she said. "Might he have fallen from the top of the cliff? Will someone say that it was just an accident waiting to happen and we did not take enough care of our guests?"

"That would be an unreasonable accusation," Clara told her. "After all, it is not up to you to constantly monitor your guests to see that they don't do something foolish. They are adults who can take care of themselves."

"I hear what you are saying, but I can't help but wonder if people will still point the finger at me. They already hate us."

"Hate is probably too strong a word," Tommy consoled her, though at the back of his mind he did consider she was right.

There were a lot of people who resented the presence of the Sun Club, and easily that resentment could turn to hate. It was amazing how people could become so volatile over someone removing their clothes.

"There is nothing to suggest this was anything more than an accident," Clara persisted. "Therefore, I don't see that we should continue investigating the case and wasting your money. I believe the most prudent thing to do now would be to contact Mr O'Brien's family and make arrangements for them to come and collect the body."

"What about the bear?" Daisy asked.

"The bear is a complication, of course," Clara nodded. "But we have no reason to suppose it's specifically hanging around your particular piece of the coast. It could be anywhere in Brighton. Dr Deáth says it may have been drawn in by the smell of blood and then slashed at Mr O'Brien intending to..."

Tommy gave his sister a hard nudge in the ribs with his elbow. She was going into too much detail; Daisy was already looking like she might faint or throw up.

"This is terrible for us," Daisy continued. "I can't see how we can carry on after this."

"Don't be so defeatist," Tommy told her firmly. "You have done nothing wrong."

"How are your other guests taking things?" Clara asked.

Daisy shrugged her shoulders.

"Two have already left, but that was to be expected. They were rather shaken up by the news. The others are hanging on. They are more stoic, perhaps, also, there aren't that many places you can go to when you are inclined towards the naturist movement, and they want to see us flourish. It's kind of them really to keep supporting us in this difficult time."

"That should give you renewed hope," Tommy told her. "To have them supporting you. I assume they are influential people in their regular day-to-day lives? That has to be what you focus on, not what people around town will say."

Daisy nodded her head.

"I suppose you're right. We should just soldier on. Edward is determined enough, of course. And he's been such a rock in these difficult times."

Daisy shuffled them out the front door after that and Clara was under the impression she wanted to be alone.

They made their way to the nearest bus stop, which was in itself quite a hike, and managed to get back home in time for tea.

Captain O'Harris had been invited and he was waiting for them, flicking through the latest edition of the newspaper. He beamed brightly as Clara walked into the room and took her into a firm embrace, kissing her on the cheek and then, when he was sure that Tommy was not present, kissing her harder on the lips.

"Annie has been regaling me with some interesting information," he said, a smirk coming onto his face. "You went to the Sun Club without me."

"You didn't miss out on anything, aside from a bloody corpse," Clara raised an eyebrow at him.

O'Harris' smirk changed to a frown.

"Yes, I did hear about that. Killed by a bear?"

"Possibly, but the important thing is that the case is fully resolved," Clara promised him. "It is now just a case of convincing Mrs Wilton that she needs to allow her son to get on with his life, and to let him do whatever he chooses to do at the Sun Club."

"Edward is a naturist?" O'Harris was intrigued.

"Not just a naturist. He has helped found the Sun Club and is one of the owners. I am not sure how his mother will take that information, but I suppose she will have to get used to it."

O'Harris was deeply amused at this news. He chuckled lightly to himself.

"I am still disappointed you went without me."

"I went completely alone to have a private chat to Daisy on the first occasion, and since she ensures that visitors do not associate with the guests, you did not miss out on anything."

Clara pulled a face at him.

"Should I be jealous of the amount of interest you have in the Sun Club?"

"Absolutely not! There is truly only one person I wish to see with their clothes off."

O'Harris leaned in to kiss her neck.

At that moment Tommy appeared in the room.

"What is that on the front cover of the paper? More about this bear business?" He sounded alarmed.

O'Harris was reluctantly distracted.

"Some big game hunter is coming to town. He's all across the newspaper saying he's going to capture the bear."

Tommy grabbed up the newspaper and shook it in anger.

"Look at this nonsense. Look at it!"

In a temper he set off to putter to Annie about this new development.

As soon as he was out of sight, Clara leaned forward to Harris.

"You were explaining to me why I should not be jealous, I believe."

Chapter Seventeen

C lara and Tommy agreed they should speak to Inspector Park-Coombs the next day and discuss the matter of this bear hunt with him. It seemed ridiculous that Brighton was going to become the hub for some hunting campaign. The last thing the town needed was a load of men wandering around shooting at anything that looked remotely like a bear. It would be bad enough having professional hunters running about, but what about all the amateurs who would just grab an old shotgun out of a cupboard to give it a go? The reward was going to tempt a lot of people out of the woodwork and most of them wouldn't have the first clue as to what to do with a gun.

As they headed into town, their worst fears started to become reality. They had to go past the *Brighton Gazette* office and there they saw various men dressed in hunting attire and carrying an assortment of firearms. They had obviously all come to sign up for the bear hunt. They were putting their names down so that if they did succeed in their quest, they could immediately claim the reward.

Tommy looked gloomily at the array of hunting pieces the men carried; everything from old shotguns to professional hunting rifles. Some of the equipment looked positively antiquated and probably hadn't been fired for decades. The chances of some of the pieces even working was slim. Even if they did, there was a strong possibility they would backfire, exploding in the face of the hunter.

"I do not like this at all," Tommy said firmly. "Why isn't anyone conducting a proper search for this bear so it can be captured and returned to where it belongs?"

"I suppose the question is who would organise something like that?" Clara responded to him. "I am not sure it comes under the police's remit."

"I think it ought to, if the animal is a hazard to the public."

"That is a point. But whether the police see it like that, or rather, whether the Chief Constable sees it like that, is another matter. In any case, I don't think there's anything we can do to stop this charade."

"Look at them all in their outfits, posing around as if they are master hunters. I have never seen anything so appalling."

Tommy despised hunting. Despite owning a gundog and thus potentially being able to participate in the regular pheasant and partridge shoots at some of the grand estates, he had no desire to do so. While he could understand hunting for the necessity of eating, shooting things merely to see how many birds or beasts you could bag in a day failed to appeal to him. He saw it as both idiotic and cruel. His thoughts on fox hunting were even stronger and more than once had interfered with the local hunt when he happened to come across them while walking his own dogs. It was not unknown for him to grab up a fox that was already on its last legs from exhaustion, shove it into his coat and positively refuse to allow the hunt's hounds to get anywhere near it.

His feelings on the bear hunt were just as strong and Clara could not help but agree with him. She thought about the poor animal just trying to survive. She doubted it was any real danger to the general public, though admittedly in countries where bears were more common they could be dangerous.

The death of Mr O'Brien rather went against that notion, except she was holding onto the flimsy notion the animal had come across the man when he was already lying unconscious on the beach.

"We best hurry to Inspector Park-Coombs and have a good conversation about what's happening here," she nodded to Tommy. "I am more worried about those men walking around with guns and the potential they have to hurt someone than I am about a bear."

When they arrived at the police station, they found it for once relatively quiet. It was a calm morning, with most people's attention drawn to the newspaper offices. The desk sergeant welcomed them and informed them that the inspector was up in his office and would gladly see them. From the hints he dropped, it seemed to Clara the inspector had suffered some sort of rebuke from the Chief Constable about this bear business. Probably he could do with a sympathetic ear to make him feel better.

She and Tommy headed upstairs and knocked on the inspector's door. He invited them in and asked them to sit before his desk.

"Is it about the bear?" He said. "Tell me you have spotted it. Or at least know someone who has spotted it."

The barrage of questions came out in almost a blur. The inspector was clearly upset.

"It *is* about the bear, but not because we have found it," Clara said apologetically. "We wanted to have a discussion about what you intend to do with all these hunters running around the town trying to catch it."

The inspector was surprised by her statement.

"You know as well as I do that I can't do anything about them. They have not broken any laws. They are perfectly entitled to come along and take a potshot at this bear."

"That is simply awful," Tommy declared sharply. "It isn't right, Inspector. Why aren't we organising a proper hunt for this bear? One that sees the animal captured and returned to the owner? It's not the animal's fault that it went for a wander."

Park-Coombs looked like he might snap back at Tommy. He was clearly at the end of his own tether. But he took a deep breath and managed to exhale it quite calmly before he actually spoke.

"It is not as simple as that," he responded. "The Chief Constable and I, have had several discussions on the subject and he refuses to allow me to expend manpower on such an affair, at least not until there's a confirmed sighting of this bear, or something occurs that can be considered a police matter."

"Mr O'Brien being slashed by claws does not constitute a police matter?" Clara asked him.

"You can't convict a wild animal for murder."

"That still means you have a potentially dangerous animal wandering around Brighton, and surely it is the duty of the police to find it?" Tommy pointed out.

"The Chief Constable is of the opinion, based on the report from Dr Death that Mr O'Brien most likely fell off the cliff and hit his head. Then the bear simply stumbled across him. He therefore can console himself that we do not need to begin a search at this moment in time, and that we can wait and see what happens with these random hunters before we expend our own energy and resources. As always, we have quite a few cases on the books at this moment in time that need my immediate attention. Despite my best efforts, the Chief Constable refuses to see this bear as a police problem."

"You mean he's happy to leave it to the amateurs to sort this out for him?" Tommy said moodily. "And what if someone else does get hurt?"

"That will be another matter, but at this moment in time, apart from the incident on the beach, no one has even spotted this bear. You do know that there's even talk that it doesn't exist?"

Neither Clara nor Tommy had heard that, and they expressed their surprise at this statement.

"I have talked with the editor at the *Brighton Gazette* and apparently the newspaper story was sent to him as an anonymous tip. Since no one has actually spotted the bear, we are slightly in a conundrum as to whether it exists. No one has come forward to give a name for the owner of the missing bear, and we have contacted all the regular zoos and private collections that we can think of and confirmed that their bears are safe and sound."

"That just means that whoever owned this bear probably did so illegally and is now trying to hide the fact that they have lost it," Clara pointed out.

"Indeed. But it also raises the possibility that this is some sort of hoax, that there isn't a bear at all."

"That doesn't explain the slash marks on Mr O'Brien," Tommy reminded him. "If there's no bear, how did that occur?"

"Dr Deáth has suggested that they might have been caused by something else. In fact, he is less convinced today than he was yesterday that they are claw marks."

This was further news to Tommy and Clara. They glanced to each other and then back at the inspector.

"He has a new theory?" Clara asked.

"Nothing in particular, but he's wondering if they could be

a coincidental injury from falling down the cliff," Park-Coombs explained. "He's wondering if Mr O'Brien scratched his chest on some rocks as he went down, and the injuries just happened to look similar to claw marks."

"Has anyone looked to see if there was blood on the cliff face?" Tommy asked.

"Not as yet. As you know, the land is private and since we have not confirmed that there has been any foul play the owners are reluctant to allow us to investigate further. More to the point, Dr Deáth is now certain that the slash marks had nothing to do with the man's demise."

"Really?" Clara asked, wondering how he had come to this conclusion.

"Though it was quite clear the man had bled to death, after further investigation it seemed to him that the man's wounds would not, under normal circumstances, have resulted in such a dramatic demise. He therefore got hold of Mr O'Brien's medical records and it turned out that the gentleman had a condition that reduced his blood's ability to clot. It was not as severe as some haemophiliacs suffer. They can get a minor cut and bleed out. But it was severe enough that his wounds did not clot as quickly as they should and allowed him to bleed to death before help arrived."

This was all news to Clara and Tommy.

"And you really cannot do anything about those hunters wandering around Brighton," Tommy demanded, his mind rapidly switching away from the tragedy that had befallen Mr O'Brien.

"I really cannot do anything about them," Inspector Park-Coombs replied. "Not unless they do something to put a person's life in danger and I very much doubt that will happen."

Chapter Eighteen

Everyone was talking about the bear hunters after that. It even went so far as for a hunter to appear down the alley behind the Fitzgeralds' house. Apparently he had heard about the supposed sighting of a bear in a backyard. Annie was present at the time; she had been feeding her chickens and she heard a commotion just outside the garden gate. She went to investigate, being cautious when she opened the gate in case there was a bear suddenly standing out there. She would not usually confront a wild animal, but when it came to her chickens, she was particularly protective. Instead of a bear, she saw a middle-aged man dressed in a hunting suit. It was old fashioned with big bulbous pantaloons that went down into tightly wound gators. He had somehow managed to take a tumble. Annie found him lying on his back like an upturned beetle. Across his chest, he was clasping an old hunting rifle. Annie determined the gentleman had been attempting to look over a garden wall by standing on some old boxes that had been next to it. The boxes had given way and he had tumbled backwards. He looked slightly dazed, and so she went to offer him a hand.

Fortunately, he was embarrassed rather than hurt and refused her offer of a cup of tea, saying that he must get on with his work. He was trying to follow a potential lead that the bear had been wandering around back gardens in the area. Annie explained to him that it all been a misunderstanding and that a very large cat had been responsible; he was deeply disappointed.

The appearance of the hunter in the alley quickly spread around the neighbours and it was all anybody could talk about. Some of the maids who worked in houses nearby came to speak to Annie, concerned themselves about the potential for a bear attack. Others were romantically attracted to the notion of these gentlemen with their guns, (probably helped by certain young ladies' magazines) and were fantasising that these noble hunters would sweep a girl off her feet while rescuing her from a bear and take her to some far-flung climate to begin life anew.

Annie didn't like the way the girls were all fantasising about the hunters, or the fact all these men were wandering around with guns. The appearance of the middle-aged hunter who had fallen back with his rifle had not consoled her, especially as at one point she realised he was holding his weapon upside down and she was not entirely convinced he knew how to use it.

She now had a new worry on her mind; that Clara and Tommy, while out and about, might end up getting themselves shot, and she decided she would tell Tommy he wasn't allowed to take the dogs for a walk, at least until this matter blew over. She knew he wouldn't be impressed, and the dogs would be even less impressed, but they had to do something for their own safety.

They were all gathered in the front parlour that evening, and O'Harris was visiting again. He came most nights to spend time with

Clara. They had just finished toasting some crumpets for evening tea and were discussing the changing seasons – thinking about the forthcoming winter and what they might do for Christmas – when there was a sharp knock on the door.

"Why must people call so late?" Annie grumbled, getting up to answer it.

Tommy waved her back.

"I'll go," he said.

He wandered into the hallway, and they heard him open the front door.

"Hope it is not another one of those hunters looking for a bear that doesn't exist here," Annie grumbled. "I have had quite enough of all that talk."

She had already told them about her experience with the hunter out in the alley, but it was quite clear she would gladly tell the story again. Clara was not listening to her. Instead, she had her ears pricked for whoever was at the front door. She thought she recognised their voice.

The next moment, Tommy was back in the front room and behind him was Edward.

Edward looked distinctly worried, and Clara was sure something else had occurred at the Sun Club. She rose at once and told him to sit himself before the fire, offering him one of the recently toasted crumpets. Edward was clearly distressed, and Annie immediately went into her role as chief comforter, insisting she would make him tea and have him eat something.

"Have you argued with your mother?" Clara asked him, wondering if he had at last broken the news to Mrs Wilton about his involvement with the Sun Club.

"No, I haven't worked up the courage to do so yet," Edward replied.

"I am sorry to call on you so late. I know it is an intrusion on your privacy, but I needed to come. I didn't know who else to go to."

"Something else has occurred at the Sun Club?" Clara asked him.

Edward nodded his head.

"One of our guests claimed he saw an animal moving around in the darkness through the trees. We were going to ignore it. The animal didn't come near him after all and with everything else that was going on, we just thought we would pretend it was nothing. Then, just a couple of hours ago, Daisy was attacked."

He immediately had their close attention.

"By a bear?" Clara asked him.

Edward shook his head.

"It was a person. They came up behind her and knocked her on the back of the head. She was out for a couple of seconds and then managed to make her way to the house. You see what this means, of course. It suggests that what happened to Mr O'Brien was not an accident, and that someone is targeting people at the Sun Club."

"Slow down," Clara said. "Where did this happen?"

"Daisy had gone for a walk through the woods that skirt around the house," Edward explained.

"The same place that someone said they had spotted a bear?" O'Harris remarked. "Wasn't that somewhat careless if she suspected there was a wild animal out there, and considering what had recently happened?"

Edward seemed to be taking him in for the first time. He was aware of who Captain O'Harris was and his relationship with Clara, so he was not concerned to keep talking in front of him.

"It was for that reason Daisy went out there. Though initially she thought a bear had attacked Mr O'Brien, she now is of the opinion that the story of the bear is being spread to cause panic among people.

She even wondered if someone was playing a joke on the household to try and scare away the rest of our guests. Had I known she intended to go through the woods on her own, I certainly would have gone with her. But Daisy is single minded and very independent."

Clara had got that impression of the woman, and she had to admire her resolve. She probably would have done something similar if she were convinced that there was a hoax and wanted to prove it.

"We had no reason at that point to doubt what Dr Deáth had told us about the incident with Mr O'Brien," Edward continued. "The coroner was very kind to speak to us again earlier this afternoon and tell us about his final conclusions on what happened. He said that he was quite willing to state that Mr O'Brien had stumbled off the cliff and had fallen and hit his head. He felt the slashes across his chest were incidental. He explained about his medical condition and how that would have caused him to bleed out in a way that a regular person would not. So, you see, Daisy and I both agreed that there was nothing to worry about and that the only reason for the sighting of a bear would be because someone who was against us, had heard the gossip, and was trying to cause us a fright."

"There is certainly a potential argument for that," Clara agreed. "There is a great deal of consternation concerning this supposed bear, and yet nobody has really had a confirmed sighting of it."

"Precisely. Anyway, Daisy decided to take herself out for a walk through the woods. It wasn't dark yet, so she thought she'd be absolutely fine. She saw no sign of a bear. She was right at the farthest extent of the estate, moving through the trees, when she heard a rustling noise behind her. She turned, but saw no one, so she carried on for a while longer. That was when she heard it again. This time when she turned, she thought she glimpsed someone amongst the trees. It was definitely not a large animal. She said that it was someone who moved very lightly on their feet.

"Considering we've had issues with protests and so forth, she wondered if someone had snuck onto the estate to take a look. It could have been a journalist. There's been quite a commotion since the death of Mr O'Brien. We've had several newspaper men gathering outside the gates trying to get a closer look. Our guests have taken to confining themselves to their rooms out of concern for their privacy. In any case, Daisy made the questionable decision to go after whoever was in the woods. We've already discussed the fact that it wasn't a sensible decision. But she's a determined person and in that moment she was angry and wanted to catch who was there. She did not suspect any danger to herself.

"She hastened to the spot where she thought she had seen the person and was looking around for signs of them when someone must have come up behind her and smacked her across the back of the head with a piece from a fallen branch. As I say, she fell forward and she was unconscious for a couple of seconds, but she doesn't think it was any more than that. When she woke up, she immediately made her way back to the house."

"And she caught no sight of this person other than the glimpse through the trees?" Clara asked.

Edward shook his head.

"Clearly we have someone prowling around trying to cause trouble for us. We've already been to the police and mentioned it to them, but at this stage they say they can't do much about it, not without any evidence or an idea of who the person might have been. The inspector did send a couple of constables to search through the woods. But they found nothing. It's all been deeply disappointing."

"And naturally, you're both worried. Not only for your own safety and the safety of your guests, but about the future of the Sun Club,"

Clara understood.

"It starts to make you wonder whether there is more to these things than we initially thought, whether there is a connection between what happened to Daisy and what happened to Mr O'Brien. Maybe someone is trying to sabotage us," Edward said in a rush.

"They would have to be pretty callous to think it was reasonable to push a man off a cliff to prove their point about the moral irregularities of a naturist colony," O'Harris remarked.

"People can be savage when it comes to these things," Edward shrugged. "I'm starting to wonder just how far some of them would go."

"Do you have any particular people in mind when you say this?" Clara asked him. "It sounds almost as though you have an idea?"

Edward nodded.

"There is a particular organisation that's growing in its antagonism towards us," he explained. "They've started a protest group, and we anticipate them becoming increasingly vocal as time goes by. They are led by a local reverend who is somewhat notorious for his involvement in anything he believes is an affront to his religion and moral standards. They're the only people we could imagine who would be prepared to go that far to prove their point about us and to drive us away. We have been having problems with them for some time, but up until recently it has mainly been unpleasant letters and threats to us about legal action. All of which have been inspected by our solicitors who tell us they cannot actually do anything."

"So maybe these people have decided to take the next step and actually put some lives at risk to make their arguments heard?" O'Harris was aghast at the thought. "That sounds rather nasty."

"It is amazing how nasty people can get when it comes to questions of moral behaviour. They can see no harm in what they're doing, nor how unpleasant it is when they think they're defending traditional values," Clara mused.

"You have to keep investigating Clara," Edward told her firmly. "We cannot allow this to continue. Someone is after us, someone who is intending to do us great harm."

"Someone who was already killed," Tommy said bleakly.

Chapter Nineteen

T he following day they headed back to the Sun Club to interview
Daisy for themselves. She was bright and chipper when they
came to the house and did not seem to be any worse for wear after her
adventure. She showed them in and insisted they take tea with her.

"Edward has explained what happened to you last night," Clara
said. "But we would like to hear it in your own words. Precisely what
occurred."

"I don't suppose there is a great deal to tell you," Daisy replied
dismissively. "I went for a walk in the woods because I wanted to see
what was going on out there. One of our guests had reported a sighting
of a bear, which I completely disbelieved. However, I did wonder if an
unwelcome visitor had climbed over the wall and was now prowling
around."

"Why did you go looking for them instead of sending your
gatekeeper?" Tommy asked.

"Because I wanted to confront the person for myself," Daisy said
firmly. "No one plays me for a fool like that, and no one treats the

people around me in such a cruel manner. I was going to give them a piece of my mind and that's the simple answer."

"Did you find anybody out in the woods?" Clara asked.

"No, at least not anybody obvious. I heard someone behind me a couple of times, but the rustling, well, it could have been just an animal. Eventually I thought I saw where the person was hiding, and I ran to the spot. There was no one there and that's when I got knocked on the back of my head."

"And you are sure that there was a person there? It wasn't just an accident, that you might have walked back into a low hanging branch?" Tommy clarified.

"I was definitely struck by someone behind me. I sensed them just before I was hit. When I recovered and looked around me, I saw the piece of wood they had used. I didn't bring it back, though in hindsight perhaps I should have done. Would it have told you anything?"

"I doubt it," Clara reassured her. "I don't suppose you can get fingerprints off a piece of wood. But it is curious what occurred here, and especially the method of attack, considering what happened to Mr O'Brien."

Daisy was nodding.

"Dr Deáth did seem pretty certain that the head injury he suffered had occurred when he fell from the cliff, but I can't help but wonder whether he was struck first and that is why he fell. It is one thing for someone to be wandering around the grounds intent on upsetting my guests by pretending to be a bear, and quite another for them to actually cause physical harm to someone. I never supposed that was going to be the case, which is why I went into the woods on my own without fear."

Daisy looked glum as she repeated this. Though she was largely recovered from the incident the afternoon before, she still had a throbbing headache and was pale from the shock. The blow had not been sufficient to warrant the need for bandages, but it had left her with a nasty bruise and a graze. She had not slept well that night. So many things on her mind and the pain throbbing around her skull.

"There is a part of me that wonders whether we should continue this at all," she said solemnly. "Maybe we should cut our losses and call it quits."

"That would seem a shame, to allow such people to get away with what they are doing," Clara said gently.

"I don't want anybody to get hurt for the sake of my naturist beliefs," Daisy replied. "It isn't worth it. I would fight this if the only bother were people throwing words and insults at us. When it comes to people being actually physically harmed, then I have to draw a line."

"That is a sensible decision," Tommy nodded to her. "But don't do anything hasty. We might be able to resolve this without you having to go so far as to close down the Sun Club."

"I am very grateful for your support," Daisy told them. "Even though I know you're not naturists, you have been very understanding of our lifestyle. You've not judged us, and for that I really do appreciate you."

"As far as we are concerned, you are causing no harm to anyone," Clara replied. "Whether you choose to wear clothes or not, it doesn't matter to anyone else."

Daisy smiled at her, and it seemed the first drop of good news she had had that day.

"Can you do anything to help us, then?" She asked.

"We can make some inquiries, see if we can find out who would have struck you."

"I'm sorry to say that is probably quite a long list of people," Daisy mused. "We've had all the usual protestors, plus some of the local lads who think it funny to climb over the wall and try to see someone naked. We've had journalists wandering around both from the local press and from the nationals trying to take photographs, which is quite frankly disgusting. They question our morality and then they try and get pictures of us nude! What does that say about them?"

"Indeed," agreed Tommy. "The press have always been good at double standards. However, I don't think a local youth who happened to climb in to get a peek at a naked body or even a journalist would go so far as to attack you. They would have run away. They had plenty of opportunity."

Daisy considered his suggestion.

"You have a point. It seems to me that whoever was in the woods deliberately hung around and followed me. Do you suppose that means they were specifically after me?"

"I wouldn't start thinking along those lines just yet," Clara consoled her. "It could be that they were waiting for anyone from the Sun Club to assault and it just happened that you were the one who came across them."

"Well, I'm glad it was me rather than one of my guests," Daisy sighed. "I can live with being banged across the head, but if something had happened to another one of my visitors, that would truly be the end of us. I'm still not sure we can weather this storm."

"You will if we can find out who is behind this and have them brought to justice," Clara told her firmly. "Now, aside from journalists and local youths trying to get a glance of the people here, what about these protestors you told us about?"

"Oh yes, they are a more serious matter," Daisy nodded. "They are a group of about a dozen people led by the Reverend Lane. He is quite an old-fashioned vicar even by the standards of the conservative

Christians around here. He preaches a good deal about damnation. When we first received letters from him about the Sun Club, it was before we had even opened. I made discreet enquiries about him. It is always prudent to know who you are up against.

"I had tried to keep word of what we were going to do here as quiet as possible, but we were getting the place ready and interviewing people for employment. The news was bound to get out. Not to mention that there had to be subtle advertisements placed to allow people to know what was going on. Sooner or later Reverend Lane was going to hear about us.

"He wrote to the council demanding they do something to stop us, which they could not because we were not doing anything wrong. He tried to claim we were going to make a nuisance or be a public morality issue. Again, the council ignored him. I am on very good terms with their planning department, having had to consult them on a couple of things.

"When his direct route to the council failed, he started to send more and more disgusting letters to us, calling me all manner of names. I don't want to repeat them. I have all the letters and I can show them to you if you wish. I thought it prudent to keep them in case there was ever any bother. By and large, I've been ignoring them, though he has stopped me in the street once or twice to berate me, and more recently he has taken to writing further letters that appear in the *Brighton Gazette*. Frankly, this is something that I was expecting and so I have not taken it terribly serious up to now."

"Yet it is not just the Reverend?" Tommy remarked. "You say he has a protest group?"

"Yes, about a dozen people. I imagine they are from his congregation. They are loyal supporters and will do whatever he says. They write letters too. I believe they have also been harassing the council about the matter. Once or twice, I've seen people hanging around outside the gate who I suspect are from this little protest group, and my gatekeeper has told me they have attempted to get in before now. Mainly they are middle-aged ladies with a lot to say for themselves. It is remarkable how militant such people can get over morals."

"Have any of these threats suggested violence?" Clara asked.

"They have never mentioned physical harm," Daisy admitted. "A lot of it has been suggestions that we're endangering our immortal souls, that we're going to hell, and so forth. To be honest, it's become so predictable, I don't even look at them now. I just put them in a drawer to save them for a later date. I fully anticipated that eventually this would all blow over and something else would distract the reverend. Once he realised, he could not do anything to us, I hoped he would just leave us alone."

Clara fancied that was a rather naïve stance. People who were as volatile and opinionated as the Reverend Lane sounded, typically did not give in so easily. They were also the sort of people who could take things to the extreme to get their point across, especially when they felt that the authorities were ignoring their protests.

"Have you any reason to suppose that the Reverend Lane has been on the grounds?" Clara asked next.

"I have never seen him, if that's what you're stating, but of course you can ask my gatekeeper. Obviously, the walls are not impenetrable if you can climb."

Daisy frowned as she considered what Clara was suggesting.

"Surely a man of the cloth would not go so far as to strike me or to hurt Mr O'Brien to make his point?"

"Being a man of the cloth has nothing to do with it," Tommy answered. "People are still people."

Daisy shook her head and then regretted it as the headache rung around her temples and she felt slightly lightheaded.

"You will look into this for me, won't you?" She asked them urgently.

"We certainly will," Clara promised her. "We will obviously have to speak to Reverend Lane. Find out what he was doing yesterday. As for you, Daisy, I suggest you keep your guests inside the house as much as possible and have your gatekeeper keep his eyes peeled."

"I have already considered that possibility," Daisy admitted. "I don't like it, but I think we have to take defensive actions while we can. I can't afford another guest being hurt."

"We shall go and take a look around the woods," Clara explained. "And see if we can spot anything that the police might have missed."

"Thank you," Daisy said with relief. "Edward assured me you would help us. He's been so worried about me."

"Edward is a good friend to you," Clara said carefully.

Daisy blushed.

"I cannot put anything past you. We are more than friends and have been for some time. We are kindred spirits, sharing our belief in the naturist cause. We do intend to marry, one day. There's nothing improper about our relationship. Just because we like to take our clothes off doesn't mean we're completely immoral."

"I believe you, Daisy," Clara promised her. "And we will do everything we can to help you."

With Daisy's gratitude still ringing in their ears, they headed out into the grounds and towards the wooded area near the wall. The grounds seemed quiet that day with only the noises of the birds in the trees. There was no sign of the gardener, and the gatekeeper was safely ensconced in his little hut down by the gates. The clouds above were grey and there was a hint of rain forming. Clara suspected they would get wet before they had finished their search.

The woods were not vast. They were the remains of an older forest that had been cut down when the estate was walled off. There was not much old timber left in it and a lot of new pines had been planted to compensate for the older trees that had been taken down. They wandered among them, looking for any signs that a person had been there. The ground was quite dry, and it did not take the impressions of feet very well, so there was no point looking for footprints.

Daisy had given them a vague idea of where she had encountered her attacker. Even so, they were surprised when they actually came across the precise spot she had described and identified it by a lump of wood they found lying on the ground with a small amount of blood on it. They were not far from the boundary wall.

"Person could have jumped over the wall, struck Daisy, and jumped back over again," Tommy remarked.

"Yes. We have no idea why they were here or why they decided to attack her."

Clara had picked up the piece of wood, now she dropped it again.

They headed to the boundary wall to take a closer look. It was at least a century old and some of the bricks had worn away, leaving convenient footholds. It would not be difficult for a person to find a way over the wall if they were nimble enough.

"I think our likeliest suspects are those involved in Reverend Lane's protest group," Clara said as they examined the wall and considered how easy it would be to get over it. "It does not even have to be someone directly involved with them, but someone who has taken up the idea. You get all sorts of crazy people who suddenly think these things are a good idea."

"Yes, it could be a single individual who just thinks they are doing what is right and has got themselves all churned up about this naturist society," Tommy concurred. "I am not entirely certain how we will actually resolve this."

"We ask questions. That's what we always do well," Clara reminded him. "In the meantime, it wouldn't hurt to see if we can get some sort of protection going for Daisy. I don't like to think of her here all alone with just Edward. The grounds are vast, and that ageing gatekeeper is not going to be up to much if someone truly wants to hurt her or her guests."

"The police don't have the resources to offer her any protection," Tommy pointed out.

"Then maybe we have to offer our own protection," Clara replied. "If we were to stay here, we could at least keep an eye on what was happening and maybe catch the perpetrator in the act."

Tommy was unsure about this idea.

"I don't think Annie will like this very much."

"I'm sure O'Harris would be delighted to help us," Clara was amused. "And if we can persuade Annie that she wouldn't see anybody without their clothes on, she would no doubt come too. I just feel we need some more people in the house who are on Daisy's side. I don't like to think that she's out here all alone with just the guests. Edward has to keep going back to his mother after all and checking on her, otherwise Mrs Wilton will have her own nervous fit."

"Maybe we should bring her here," Tommy said with a grimace. "She could scare off most people. If anyone was going to be good at preventing a vicar from getting into the grounds, it would surely be her. They would stay clear just to avoid hearing her talking on the subject of the immorality of the naturist movement."

Clara smirked at his joke. It was true that Mrs Wilton's opinions often could confuse the most obsessed of individuals and cause them to reassess their own views.

"Leaving Mrs Wilton out of it," Clara said, knowing it would not be wise to inflict her on Daisy, "we should go home and have a talk with Annie and convince her to come here just until we can get a better idea of what's going on, and who might be behind these crimes. In the meantime, we ought to go and have a chat with this Reverend Lane and find out just how far he would go to promote his own beliefs."

Chapter Twenty

The Reverend Lane lived in a decrepit Victorian Vicarage, down an equally decrepit lane that was lined with ageing Beech trees. His property was dark and gloomy, built at the end of the Victorian era primarily in the style of the Gothic movement. It was most likely rather damp to reside in. It had a gloomy, dark brown veranda that ran around the outside of the property that was supposed to give some sort of place to sit in the glorious days of summer, but instead cast long shadows over the windows and made it seem as if the house was huddling in on itself, glaring at the world around it.

Clara wondered if houses tended to influence the people who lived there, or if it was the other way around, whether a person who was of a gloomy and dark disposition was drawn to such a property, and made it seem gloomy and dark because of their presence.

After all, the Reverend Lane would have been given this property when he took over the local church. He could not be accused of creating it, asking it to be built in such a fashion. He had just inherited the property from whoever had lived in it before. Clara had to surmise it did not say much for the abilities of the Church of England architects, if they could create such a place. It did not look particularly welcoming or one that would draw in the spiritually speculative.

At that moment in time, however, that was not her concern.

She was interested in Reverend Lane's complaints about the Sun Club and why he had taken so against it. In particular, she was curious to see if he seemed the sort of gentleman who would be prepared to go to any lengths to get his way. Hurting people was extreme, but sometimes people who were indignant did extreme things, even when their calling should have made them pacifist in their tendencies and opposed to violence against others.

Clara was used to people being contradictory in their nature. Very little surprised her these days. Reverend Lane proved to be among those things that did not surprise her. When they knocked on the door, he answered it himself. He was an older gentleman wearing a beige cardigan with hair that was going slightly wild and bushy eyebrows. He looked as though he should really be considering retirement, but Clara suspected he was one of those clergymen who could not resist the temptation of remaining in their posts right until the very last. Nothing would get him to step away from his calling other than death itself.

Such was the case with an awful lot of Church of England clergymen, and she had no doubt it was even worse in the Catholic Church, where posts were certainly for life. It must be frustrating for those who were younger, trying to rise up the ranks and who wanted a proper place where they could make their mark, but were stymied by the fact that older gentlemen were holding on to those places with dogged determination.

Reverend Lane looked at them through a pair of dark spectacles. The glass had been tinted, perhaps to help shield his eyes from the sunshine, though on a day like today, Clara imagined it made the dark house seem even gloomier.

He did not greet them immediately. He peered at them as if he were trying to assess who they might be and why they were there. It was clear that he was not used to receiving strangers. He expected to know whoever was standing on his doorstep and the fact he did not recognise either Clara or Tommy was giving him cause for concern.

Finally, and perhaps somewhat reluctantly, he remembered his manners.

"What can I do for you?"

"You are the Reverend Lane?" Clara asked him carefully.

"I am."

He assessed them again through those glasses, now trying to work out why they might suddenly be on his doorstep. Clara revised her earlier opinion; she now had the impression that the Reverend Lane quite frequently received people who were not happy with him and was probably inclined to be very cautious to whom he spoke.

"We just popped along so we could have a talk about the Sun Club," Clara said to him, keeping her statement vague enough to allow him to make his own interpretation.

As she had hoped, the reverend immediately jumped to the wrong conclusion. Or rather, he jumped to the conclusion she wanted him to jump to.

"Ah, you are here to complain about the moral outrage of the Sun Club too," he said, assuming that anybody who came to his doorstep and was fully clad must be opposed to the place.

"We have heard about your movement," Clara said, without answering his question. "And we wanted to come and meet you."

"I am always glad to have new additions to the group," Reverend Lane said, now looking quite cheerful. He was no longer glowering at them over his tinted glasses or hunching his shoulders like he was some humanoid vulture. "You must come in. It's my housekeeper's day off, but I can make a perfectly adequate cup of tea myself. I think I can even find some biscuits."

They followed the reverend into the house and were led through to a parlour at the back. Reverend Lane seemed keen to talk about the Sun Club. He was enthusiastic about his stance against it, gabbling out details as they walked along the corridor.

"I'm glad to see that other young people are becoming involved in the concerns about this immoral and desperate situation," he said. "Miss Belle has not taken any of my protests seriously. I have attempted to be moderate and polite in my behaviour towards her, but she does not return the gesture. She has positively declined to speak to me about anything that is going on within that house of sin. I am determined to see the place shut down."

Clara wondered just how determined the reverend would be. How far would such a man go?

Once the reverend had gone off to make the tea, they took a closer look around the parlour to try and get a feel for the man. They took note that his bookshelves were filled with ecclesiastical texts, though this in itself did not necessarily mean much, for any man who was of the cloth and who regularly wrote sermons would certainly have such a collection to assist him with his work.

There was nothing in the parlour that immediately told them that Reverend Lane was the sort of person to knock unarmed women on the back of the head. When he at last returned with the tea, Clara decided to be cautious about how she questioned him.

"I brought you one of my printed pamphlets," Lane said excitedly, putting down a piece of paper before them. "I wrote it myself and distribute them among as many people as I can."

The flimsy piece of folded paper was crudely printed on one of the old-fashioned mechanical copiers that people could employ for such means. The ink was smeared and some of the letters not fully formed.

Clara picked up the pamphlet and examined it carefully. The wording was not much better than the printing in terms of its quality. There were a lot of sharp and bold statements, such as Stop the Nudity. Crackdown on immorality. Think of your children.

There was very little in the way of logical argument laid out in the pamphlet. It was the sort of thing Clara expected from such a man as Lane. He was good for making a broad statement and spinning a good line, but anything that equated to something sensible or detailed was beyond him.

Clara returned the pamphlet to the table before them and smiled at the reverend.

"I hear you lead the protest group that is arguing against the Sun Club's presence," she said.

"I do indeed. I founded it among my congregation initially, but I am delighted that so many other people from outside are now beginning to become involved. The thing is, you have to remind people of their moral duty and also to enlighten them as to what problems the place could cause them."

"What precisely are those problems?" Tommy asked gently.

"Well, for a start, they are inducing in the minds of our children that it is natural to wander around without any clothes on, having one's wicked way with whomever one chooses to have it with. It's sad to say that today things are pretty bleak for our youth. It is not like it was when I was a boy. Everyone was so honourable and decent. Today it's all so scandalous. You see it every day in the papers."

"But children aren't allowed at the Sun Club," Clara pointed out.

"That is hardly the point. They could see something through the gates. The very thought of that place and what goes on there could encourage them to imitate it."

"I don't think the Sun Club encourages promiscuity among its guests," Tommy added. "My understanding is that is actually frowned upon."

Reverend Lane was not impressed by this statement.

"They will say anything they think you want to hear to encourage you to support them. Do not be fooled by them. The place is a hotbed for sin. I have no doubt they are jumping from bed to bed in midnight orgies all the time."

The way Reverend Lane said this with some delight suggested to Clara that he was not entirely against the idea of midnight orgies. In fact, he almost seemed to relish the notion. He just didn't like the idea of someone else participating in them.

"The thing is, whatever they intend to do on that site, it's private land and therefore there is nothing that any of us can do about it," Clara decided to move on from Lane's preaching, she did not need to know further about why he disagreed with the Sun Club. He had made that plain enough.

"I know exactly what you are saying, young lady," Lane spoke to her, thinking she was a sympathetic ear. "I have addressed the police myself regularly and they insist on telling me that there is nothing they can do. Whatever happens on private land is perfectly allowed unless it breaks a specific law such as murder."

The use of that particular word caught Clara's attention. She glanced at Tommy.

"What an interesting thing to say," Tommy remarked, "considering what we have heard recently."

Lane raised an eyebrow at them, as if he didn't understand where they were heading.

"A gentleman died at the Sun Club, didn't he?" Tommy persisted.

"I do believe there was an incident," Reverend Lane nodded. "An unfortunate matter. Of course, the police tell me it was not murder."

"You have discussed it with them?" Clara said, intrigued by this declaration.

"I happened to speak with their inspector, yes," Lane continued. "I arrange regular meetings with him to be kept up to date with the situation at the Sun Club. I present him with any new information I feel would be relevant to him."

"I am sure he greatly appreciates that," Clara said, trying not to smirk at the thought of poor Inspector Park-Coombs being confronted by the vicar every Monday morning with a list of further grievances against the Sun Club.

"Well, anyway, I addressed him on the matter of the death at the Sun Club and he tells me it appears to have been an accident, some wild animal roaming around killed the man. I find that quite remarkable, don't you? To suppose that a bear is suddenly wandering around Brighton?"

"It seems to be the talk of the town," Tommy agreed. "There are now amateur and professional hunters going about with guns trying to shoot the beast."

"An utter disgrace," Lane snapped. "Just think what damage they could do if they shoot the wrong thing."

Tommy could easily get caught up in a discussion about the morality of allowing hunters to go after the bear willy-nilly in town. Clara quickly intercepted the conversation to prevent that happening.

"How far are you prepared to go to push the Sun Club out of Brighton?" She asked.

Lane turned his attention to her. There was a slight hint of surprise in his expression.

"How far?" He said, staring at her.

"Seeing that all you have tried already is not working, I just wandered if you are prepared to take things in another direction? I mean, you protested outside the gates, I presume, to little effect."

"We have indeed done that," Lane agreed. "As you are quite right in pointing out, nothing occurred other than that the police were called on *us*, would you believe, and we were asked to desist. I am told it is improper for us to cause so much annoyance to our neighbours. Remarkable, isn't it? What people consider improper."

"Then if all your tactics have so far failed," Clara dragged him along gently, "perhaps it is time to try something more dramatic. Say doing something that would scare the Sun Club away?"

Lane's eyes went wide.

"Are you implying we actually cause harm to the people at the Sun Club?"

"Nothing serious, of course, just something that would worry them a little and make them think twice about parading around without their clothes on," Clara continued acting in a nefarious manner that would have caused mild concern for Tommy had he not known it was a pretence. "Think about it. We just give them a nudge in the right direction. They must already be spooked by the bear attack. All we need to do is to make the guests think that there is danger to them at the Sun Club or that they could be embroiled in some sort of scandal. It would result in the Sun Club having to close down. No guests, no Sun Club."

Lane's mouth dropped open and he almost stammered as he tried to respond to the statement. His shock appeared genuine.

"I am sorry miss, but that is not my intention. I would never do anything so underhand."

"I thought you would do anything to get rid of the Sun Club," Clara protested, aiming to look as though she was hurt by his refusal.

"I would do anything that is legal and legitimate, but I would never endanger people. I fear we are running on different paths," Lane smiled to them and started to look uneasy. "It was delightful to talk to you, but I'm afraid I'm rather busy and I ought to get back to my sermon."

"We should probably attend the next meeting of your protest group," Tommy interjected into the conversation before the reverend could see them out of the house.

"Oh well..."

Clara had picked up the leaflet again.

"Why it meets tonight," she said, reading the information on the back. "We shall return later then. It will be delightful to see exactly what you are planning to do next."

"Of course," the reverend said, looking uneasily between them.

He rose to show them out of the house. The look upon his face suggested that he was most alarmed by the idea of them coming back later. He was glad to get them out of the door and shut it behind them. Clara and Tommy slowly walked back down the path.

"I don't think Reverend Lane is involved in any criminal activity around the Sun Club," Tommy said to his sister. "Seems to me it rather upset him to think about it."

"He is a man of words rather than actions. But that does not mean that someone else in the protest group might not have taken what he has been saying to heart."

"Naturally," Tommy nodded. "So, we shall return tonight, and mingle around and find out if any of them have violent inclinations?"

"That is exactly what we will do," Clara agreed. "And woe betide any of them who turn out to have been wandering around the Sun Club, threatening the residents."

Chapter
Twenty-One

As soon as they had returned home, Clara summoned everyone to a council of war. They had to do something to protect the Sun Club's residents and to ensure that Daisy and Edward were not further harmed. If the police were not going to involve themselves, then they would have to take matters into their own hands. Among her troops were Captain O'Harris, Private Peterson, Annie and their friend and local photographer Oliver Bankes.

Oliver had been something of a last-minute choice. He was the police photographer and also worked for the local paper. He was not the first person they would think to employ to protect someone, but he would be another set of eyes, and he certainly was up for an adventure. Clara had made it very plain that he was not to bring his camera. Oliver had attempted to look hurt that she would insinuate he would do such a thing, though, truth be told, he had been considering slipping it in to take some pictures of the inside of the Sun Club. Nothing improper, of course. He would not be so immodest as to take pictures of nude guests. But he had thought it might make for good copy for the newspaper to have images of the interior of the Sun Club. You never knew when something might come along that would require them.

They had briefly considered the possibility of including Colonel Brandt in the operation, but they had all concurred that he would probably find it too difficult. He was not as agile as he once was and certainly would not be much assistance in prowling the grounds for intruders. What he would do if he actually came across an intruder was also a cause for concern. He might end up in more danger than the guests. Not to mention, Clara was not entirely certain what he would make of the whole concept of the Sun Club, and she didn't like to put him in a situation where he might feel uncomfortable, or for that matter, where Daisy might feel uneasy about her protectors.

It was going to be difficult enough including Annie, whose thoughts on nudity and the behaviour that went on at the Sun Club - or rather the behaviour she *assumed* went on at the Sun Club - were rather draconian.

She had agreed to the matter not precisely because she wanted to be involved, but because she didn't like to think of anybody being in danger. And when it was mentioned that Edward was one of those who could be at risk, she was quick enough to agree.

She had been involved in the case that Clara had worked on where they had restored Edward to his mother, and she remembered the traumatised young man who had come back from the Front. The one who seemed to jump at shadows and didn't know if he would be welcomed back. Though Edward had moved on from that troubled young man, Annie could not help but think of him as he had once been and did not want to see any harm coming to him.

Clara had assured her that no one would go around the place naked while she was present. Not that she had discussed this with Daisy, but she was sure that they could make an accommodation for Annie. As it was, Annie was to remain in the house, keeping an eye on Daisy while the rest of them would take turns to monitor the grounds for any signs of intruders. It was going to be a lengthy operation, as far as they could see, at least until they could determine who was behind the attacks. They would have to take shifts to enable them to all have a chance to rest.

O'Harris had briefly mentioned the possibility of including the men from his home in the operation.

However, Clara did not think it would be advisable to have a lot of soldiers wandering around the Sun Club. For a start, she could not guarantee how any of them would react to the principles of the place. She did not know them well enough to be able to assess whether they would approve, disapprove or be given to lewd comments on the subject. Secondly, she felt there was a limit to how many people Daisy would accept onto the property, and if too many were around, then no intruders would actually take a chance to get into the place and that could prevent them from finding out who was behind the attack.

What she really wanted was to lure in the intruders and catch them in the act.

However, after some discussion, she did agree with Captain O'Harris that Private Peterson should be involved in the matter. Peterson was a long-term resident at the Home. He was slowly improving but was a chronic case who needed far more attention than most of the other residents. He had undergone a wealth of psychiatric treatment in various other places that had been ineffectual. Everything from electric shock therapy to water treatments had been tried to overcome his bouts of depression, hallucinations, and general relapses into the trauma of war. The only place where he'd really found that he could function in life was at the Home.

Though the goal with all of the men was to eventually get them back into regular lives, to live with their families and make some sort of future for themselves, with Private Peterson, things were somewhat different. He was able to get along while he was at the Home. It seemed to suit him with the regularity of the life there and he always had people he could turn to if he were having one of his episodes. He felt safe there, not to mention he also felt that he could bring no harm to anyone else. The trouble was, anytime he went home, he would start to develop anxiety about the fact that he was no longer among his support network, that he was effectively on his own. The longer he was away, the more this grew on him, and he started to relapse.

It was beginning to look very likely that he might become a permanent resident of the Home. No one spoke about this out loud. O'Harris did not see that there should be a limit to the amount of time a person should be given to heal, and if Peterson did need to remain at the home indefinitely, if that was how it enabled him to function, then he was prepared to give him that opportunity. He already felt the young man had improved significantly. Who was he to deny him the opportunity to continue improving, even if it took years?

Peterson would be a good asset to the team, O'Harris promised them. He could work with the captain, and he was well trained in military forms of surveillance. If there was any problem with an intruder, he would be fully able to handle the matter and get hold of them. O'Harris reminded them that they would be potentially dealing with someone of a violent nature, and it was best to have as many able bodies available to them to deal with that person as was possible.

Clara had a slight feeling that he was insinuating that he was not confident about her abilities to deal with an intruder with murderous intentions. He never said anything out loud, but there was just a hint he would be happier if either himself or Peterson accompanied her when she did her rounds.

Clara fully believed in her own ability to take down any intruder who got in her way. She decided she would have to have a discussion with O'Harris at some point, just to make it plain between them that she was not in need of being coddled or protected. Of course, she did appreciate the protection, who wouldn't? The thought of someone caring about you and wanting to keep you safe was always a pleasant experience as long as it wasn't overwhelming, and O'Harris knew to be subtle enough with his intentions to avoid making her feel stifled most of the time.

He just needed to be gently reminded that he didn't need to worry about her so much, and that Clara was quite capable of taking matters into her own hands when she needed to. That being said, it was advisable to have them go in pairs around the grounds when they were looking for trouble and having Peterson on board brought them up to an even number. No one would have to find themselves alone at any point, whether they were inside the house or outside. It was a sensible decision, and Clara was not going to argue about it.

"This is how we're going to work things," Clara said when they were all settled into the house and Peterson had been introduced to Oliver. "Tommy and I will go out this evening to infiltrate the protest group at Reverend Lane's house. The rest of you will remain at the Sun Club, where we will have already introduced you to Miss Belle and of course, Edward Wilton. I don't suppose that the meeting at Reverend Lane's house will go on for very long. While we are there, I suggest that a pair of you remain inside the house to keep an eye on the guests and, more specifically, an eye on Daisy and Edward, to make sure that they are safe, while the other pair make the rounds of the garden."

"We can arrange that simply enough," O'Harris agreed, nodding to Peterson. "I suggest we divide our time. I should take the first shift with Oliver going around the grounds, and Peterson will remain with Annie to keep an eye on the house."

Though no one had said it out loud, there had been an unspoken agreement that Annie would not be expected to wander the grounds looking for an intruder. It was not the sort of task that Annie would gladly undertake, or one they would like to put her at risk doing. For that matter, there was a question of what she might do to an intruder if they took her by surprise. Annie could be quite feisty if she felt threatened, and they had all quietly agreed that it might be prudent if she remained in the house for the sake of the intruder as much as anything.

"Annie is going to be the main person keeping an eye on Daisy," Clara added just to make it clear where Annie's duty would lie. "I think it would be best if myself and Annie divide this task between us. Daisy is unlikely to be so keen to have men lingering around her at all times."

Clara did not actually know if this were true, but it did make it easier to convince Annie that she would be best placed in the house. Otherwise, she might have got it into her head that she would trundle off with Tommy to offer him back up when he was on his patrol. And Clara had no doubt that Annie *would* protect Tommy while they were out patrolling. She just would prefer it if any of the suspects they came across were returned to the house in one piece and capable of answering questions.

"With any luck, this operation will not need to last long. In fact, if we can narrow down a list of suspects while we're at the meeting with the reverend, we may not need to do much more. I shall also speak to Daisy plainly about looking at her own security measures and how she might make it more challenging for an intruder to get into the grounds. If we can agree to confine everybody into the house at night, that in itself would assist us."

"Just what do you suppose an intruder might do next?" Peterson asked quietly.

There would have been a time when he would not have been prepared to voice a question among them, but he had grown in confidence. Clara was delighted to hear him speaking up.

"Quite honestly, I don't know," she responded to him. "So far we know that they have been prepared to strike Daisy on the head and injure her. Did they intend to cause her serious harm or just to make sure that she was unconscious while they made their escape? We don't know, and we also don't know why they were on the site in the first place. There could be a lot of reasons for it, of course."

"I haven't ruled out the possibility that we could be dealing with an errant hunter who was looking for the bear," Tommy added. "It's been in all the newspapers that a man was attacked on the beach down below the Sun Club. It would make logical sense for one of the hunters to come there and try and track the animal. Perhaps they were spooked by being spotted on private land and didn't want to be recognised as a trespasser and panicked."

"Then the matter might not be to do with the Sun Club at all," O'Harris nodded his head in agreement. "But of course, we can't rule out anything at this point in time."

"We have to assume that the intruder meant to cause trouble for the Sun Club. I think that is most prudent," Clara added. "I feel that if it was a hunter who had come to the site, they wouldn't have been so quick to disappear. They would have tried to talk their way out of the situation. But of course, we do not know for sure what is going on and so we have to be careful. Our goal is not to chase off the intruder, but to capture them so that we can talk to them and find out what is really going on."

"The sooner they talk, the sooner I can get back to my kitchen," Annie said, and her manner of voice suggested that she would employ any means to succeed in that task.

"Whatever we do, the important thing is that we try not to alert the guests to what we're up to at this moment in time. They are under the impression that there has been an unfortunate accident on the beach that was outside of the control of the Sun Club. We don't want them to suppose that anything worse could happen or that someone is deliberately targeting the place."

Annie made a huffing noise, as if she didn't really think it mattered if they upset the guests at the Sun Club. Clara gave her a sharp look.

"That means we all have to keep our tongues firmly in our mouths and not say anything that could compromise the situation. Understood?"

Clara's gaze fell firmly on Annie who returned it with an equally stern look.

"Just let it be known," she said coolly. "That there shan't be cake in the larder while I have to go on this operation, I certainly won't have the time to make it. And don't expect scones for a while either."

Tommy grimaced. Clara, however, tried to hide a smile. Annie's attempt to punish them with a withdrawal of food indicated just how she felt about the operation, but it did at least mean she was prepared to engage with it.

"Now we all know what we ought to do," Clara said to them. "First things first we have dinner, and then we set out to protect the Sun Club."

Chapter
Twenty-Two

O'Harris had brought his car, so it was easy enough for him to give Clara and Tommy a lift to the end of the lane down which the reverend had his home, and then to carry on to the Sun Club. Daisy was expecting her new guests and protectors. Clara foresaw there would be no bother for them to set themselves up at the house while she and Tommy got on with the meeting.

The gloomy vicarage looked somewhat more enticing with lights on in the windows. It couldn't be called picturesque, but it certainly looked as though it was welcoming them in rather than trying to turn them away. While there were no other cars around the entrance, there were several bicycles and when Clara and Tommy approached the door, they could hear people speaking. The noise was quite loud; easy to hear over the general quiet of the surrounding landscape. They knocked on the door and were greeted this time by an older woman. She was a rounded, cheery sort of person, wearing an apron and a cap, and she happily showed them into one of the front rooms, where there was a gathering of guests.

Clara took note of half a dozen people who were gathered in the space taking tea and biscuits, with the Reverend Lane forming the seventh person. He glanced up at their arrival and from the look on his face it appeared that he had hoped they were not going to make an appearance. They were slightly late for the meeting, and he had probably hoped they had forgotten all about it. Despite his disdain for their presence, he pushed a smile onto his face and walked over to them.

"A pleasure to see you again," he said, offering a hand to Tommy and then to Clara, which did at least put him up in her estimation. Very few men offered to shake her hand, even though in these modern times it was far more acceptable than it once would have been.

"I was not sure if you were going to make it," the reverend said, trying to pretend he was very glad they had.

"I would not miss this for the world," Clara told him with a broad smile. She was already taking a look around the room, eyeing up the guests and trying to work out if any of them looked like the sort who would steal over a wall into a private garden.

At first glance, there did not look to be an obvious suspect among the group which consisted of four women and two men. The women ranged in age from around twenty to somewhere in their sixties. While both men were somewhere in their forties. The women were well dressed and looked as though they had some money to spare. They also did not look like the sort of people who would scurry over a brick wall, at least not in the skirts they were wearing. Clara mentally noted to herself that the youngest probably had the fitness to do something like that. She ruled out the oldest, who was carrying a stick in one hand, and leaned on it heavily as she moved about the room. The way she dragged her foot suggested she had some condition that permanently affected her ability to walk.

Of the two men, one looked like a bumbling clerk. He wore thick glasses and was rotund. He appeared to be constantly on the precipice of dropping his cup of tea. He was trying his best to hide away from the group, keeping back and listening in on the conversation without becoming involved. If anyone spoke to him, he would duck his head and mumble into his tea, overcome by shyness. While Clara could not rule out that he might be driven to assault Daisy, she had to admit, he did not look the likeliest of suspects. That left one other man.

Though of a similar age to the first man, he was marking the years far more handsomely. He stood tall with a military bearing, wore a sharp suit, and had an elegant moustache. His dark hair had been neatly oiled back and he had an intense and intelligent gaze that he directed immediately on Clara as she entered the room.

She sensed she was being assessed, though exactly for what reason she was not sure. She determined that of all the people there, this man seemed the one who could have the inclination and also the ability to make it into the grounds of the Sun Club.

"I suppose I better introduce you," Reverend Lane said uneasily. Quite clearly he would prefer it if he didn't have to introduce them at all. "Let me see. We have Miss and Mrs Harper, Miss Soaper, and Mrs Melton, all of whom are members of my congregation. Then we have Mr Drake and Mr Plainer.

As the reverend did not suggest that these two gentlemen were members of his congregation, Clara assumed that they were connected with the protest group by other means.

"Ah, I don't appear to know your names to return the introductions," Reverend Lane said looking self-conscious as he realised he had failed to get their names at their previous meeting.

"Miss and Mr Fitzgerald," Clara explained. "We are brother and sister."

It was a risk giving their real names because some people knew who they were and about their detective business, but there were no signs of recognition among anybody apart from Mr Plainer, who looked at Clara with some degree of surprise. She wondered if he had heard her name before.

"Delightful to have you here," Lane replied, still trying to hide his nervousness. "Can I offer you a cup of tea?"

They were both happy to accept the beverage, and then they split up to begin circulating around the room and talking with the other people present. Clara immediately turned her attention to Mr Plainer. She wandered over to him in a casual way and began engaging him in conversation.

"Are you a member of Reverend Lane's congregation?"

"No," Mr Plainer replied. "I'm afraid I do not regularly attend church."

"Then how do you come to be here?" Clara asked him politely.

"I own a property not far down the road from the Sun Club," Plainer explained. "It was brought to my attention what was going on there by the Reverend, who suggested I might be interested in coming to the meetings here and learning more. I deemed that appropriate."

His stuffy manner and formality suggested Clara was not going to get much from him, but she was determined to persist.

"You are concerned that they may lower the neighbourhood's tone?" She asked.

"I am concerned that we are encouraging people of low moral character to come to our neighbourhood. Who knows what they will get up to? Perhaps they will begin wandering along the roads without their clothes on, upsetting the neighbours and, of course, the local shopkeepers."

"I very much doubt they will do that," Clara said, smiling to herself at the thought of any of the members of the Sun Club being prepared to do such a thing, they were more scared about scandal than these people were.

"It's simply not the sort of thing someone wants near their home," Mr Plainer continued.

"Naturally," Clara responded. "Where, precisely, is your house?"

"Lochdale Manor is just a mile from the Sun Club," Mr Plainer remarked. "I am in the process of renovating it for the purposes of selling it on. I inherited it, you see, and I do not need the place myself. I am not really taken by the countryside."

"Ah, but I see your concerns," Clara commented. "If you wish to sell this property, then having the Sun Club so nearby could be detrimental to that end."

"You understand me perfectly," Mr Plainer nodded. "I have to take into account my own situation and how the Sun Club could be a problem to me. It is simply not right that Miss Belle has decided to open the place just when I'm about to start the proceedings for selling my property. She knows full well what I have at stake here."

Clara thought that was a loaded statement, and so she decided to pry a bit more.

"What do you have at stake?"

Mr Plainer did not want to speak more on the subject; however, he had already said too much because he had been roused by his own indignation. He made a fuss about the fact that his tea had gone cold and that he really could do with another cup. He then abandoned Clara to go over and serve himself from the fresh teapot the housekeeper had just brought into the room.

Clara supposed she had quite a good motive for Mr Plainer choosing to go into the grounds of the Sun Club and causing trouble. If he needed the sale of the house soon, for the sake of his financial situation, then certainly it made a good deal of sense that he might be inclined to cause trouble. However, motive alone was not going to take her very far, and she could not say if he was likely to steal onto the grounds and strike someone on the head.

She was thinking she would turn her attention to the only other male in the room likely to be capable of such a thing, when she glanced up and noted that Mr Drake had slipped away. He was now in the corner of the room, seemingly trapped in a conversation with the elderly Mrs Melton. The way she was tapping the floor with her stick and thrusting her finger at Drake suggested he was not going to escape anytime soon. The small amount of terror on his face as he was presented with the woman's arguments further made Clara wonder if he was actually even capable of such a thing as striking an unarmed woman. He looked as though he was afraid of his own shadow.

Tommy had struck up a conversation with the Harpers. Clara turned her attention to the only other person who was not currently engaged. That was Miss Soaper, a woman who was tall and elegant but tended towards being overly thin, to the point where it was possible to see far too much of her bones through her clothing. Her outfit hung on her, accentuating her sharp, pointed shoulders and elbows. The fashion was currently to be flat chested among women and Miss Soaper certainly had no issues in that regard. Her lack of the normal feminine curves went so far as to make her seem emaciated. Clara also noted that she did not appear to be eating any of the biscuits, cake, or sandwiches that the housekeeper had brought in.

She wandered over to the woman and smiled at her.

"Miss Fitzgerald," she said.

"Miss Soaper," Miss Soaper responded. "It is a pleasure to have some new faces at our meeting."

"We only recently learned about the Sun Club," Clara explained, telling the truth. "How many more members of the protest group are there, aside from those who are here?"

A half smile quirked the edge of Miss Soaper's mouth.

"This is pretty much it," she said.

"Oh, I was under the impression that it was a larger group. At least that's what I understood when we spoke originally to Reverend Lane."

"The good reverend does tend to make things sound bigger than they are," Miss Soaper said with a smile. "But this is really all we are. Four women from his congregation and the two men who have *interests* in the neighbourhood, shall we say?"

"I understand that Mr Plainer has a house he wishes to sell, and he fears that its value will be diminished by having the Sun Club too close," Clara nodded.

"Unfortunately, Mr Plainer only ever thinks about money," Miss Soaper responded. "That is the only reason he is here. Quite frankly, if he could find a buyer for that house who would gladly pay more to be near the Sun Club, he would quickly enough turn tail and leave us."

"What about the poor fellow cowering before Mrs Melton?"

"Mr Drake is a curious fellow. His interest in the Sun Club and seeing its demise has nothing to do with property or morality."

Miss Soaper was clearly enjoying leading Clara along with this vague statement.

"You certainly have my interest now," Clara remarked. "What precisely is Mr Drake's concern with the Sun Club?"

"Mr Drake's concern is of a personal nature," Miss Soaper persisted. "As such, I am not sure whether I should say anything more."

"Come now, you have said this much, and you clearly want to tell me what this is all about. We are all here for the same reason."

"Now that is a statement I simply cannot ignore. We are not all here for the same reason. For instance, I have no idea why you are here.

Just because Reverend Lane has said that you were willing to protest against the Sun Club potentially means nothing."

"You have a fair point," Clara agreed. "But I suspect you did not stoke my curiosity simply to just turn aside and say nothing more."

That mischievous smile crept across Miss Soaper's lips again. Clearly it entertained her to be so frustratingly secretive.

"Let me put it this way, Mr Drake knows someone at the Sun Club."

"Well, that is interesting," Clara said. "Do you mean he knows one of the guests and is that why he is here? Does he disapprove of that person being involved?"

"I'm not sure if he disapproves or not of the interests of the Sun Club," Miss Soaper said in that sideways fashion that was becoming quite irritating. "But I do know he wants to see the place closed down."

"You have me more confused than ever," Clara spoke. "He does not disapprove of the place, yet he wants it shut down?"

Miss Soaper was clearly enjoying tormenting Clara and gradually feeding her this information. Clara decided she had had enough and would try a different tactic. If Miss Soaper was really the gossip that she thought she was, she would not appreciate it if her latest listening post decided they had had enough.

"I think I best go rescue my brother from the Harpers," Clara said, taking a step away from Miss Soaper.

At the risk of losing a person who had yet to come across the information she held, Miss Soaper immediately reacted.

"The person he knows is Miss Daisy Belle," she said.

This instantly caught Clara's attention and drew her back, which was exactly what the woman wanted.

"Miss Belle?" She said. "Mr Drake knows her?"

"More than knows her," Miss Soaper was delighted to have Clara's full interest back on her. "At one time they were engaged to be wed."

Chapter
Twenty-Three

Annie took a long look around the room she had been led into. She had half expected to see some dubious drawings; pictures of scantily clad men and women cavorting in all sorts of rampant scenes of sexual misconduct. What she actually saw was a series of watercolour paintings of views around Brighton. There was not a glimpse of a nude person in any of them. In fact, they were all quite conservative. The room itself was neatly appointed and was not anything like she might have imagined. She had visions of luxurious red velvet furnishings. The sort of thing you might imagine turning up in a brothel. Instead, this room was furnished in light floral patterns, and everything was slightly old-fashioned.

Having surveyed the room and come to the conclusion that it was designed that way to lead one into a false sense of security, she prepared to meet Daisy. Captain O'Harris, Private Peterson, and Oliver were all with her, waiting to meet the lady of the house. They had been shown into the room by Edward himself. He was now pouring them out drinks from a cabinet to one side of the room. Annie had declined anything alcoholic, but the three gentlemen were quite glad to accept.

Just as Edward was handing drinks to Captain O'Harris and Private Peterson, a lady swept into the room. Daisy was wearing her most flamboyant of outfits; one that consisted of flowing loose robe-like garments, coordinated with garish jewellery in gold and red, most of which was glass and paste. What she was not, was scantily clad. In fact, Annie would be surprised if she were not wearing at least three layers of clothing. The shawl that she had over her shoulders was floor length and made of the lightest of fabrics so that you could see through it to the clothing below. Underneath was a cardigan made of some shimmering material that came to her waist, and beneath that was an elegant dress that came down in pleats to below her ankles.

Although the outfit was clearly decadent in its decoration and perhaps not the sort of thing you would go out walking in, it could hardly be described as being risqué. There was not a hint of naked skin showing, aside from Daisy's hands and her face. The cardigan came right down to her wrists and the shawl masked most of her neck.

Again, Annie assumed this was a means of drawing them in, to convince them that there was nothing morally questionable about this place. She did not lower her guard. She was not going to give them the benefit of the doubt. Not yet, anyway.

"Thank you all for coming," Daisy moved forward and offered her hand to Captain O'Harris first. He returned the gesture, and she continued around the room, shaking the hands of Private Peterson, Oliver, and finally, Annie.

"Clara has said I have nothing to worry about while you all here," Daisy continued.

"That is quite true," Captain O'Harris said, taking the lead. "We shall keep a surreptitious eye on the grounds in case of any more intruders, and there will always be someone inside the house just in case."

"I will feel a lot better for the company. Edward and I are agreed that we are starting to feel very isolated out here."

"We are trying to keep as much from the guests as possible," Edward interjected. "Which means we cannot involve them in our concerns. Once they are up in their rooms at night it is just me and Daisy, and it starts to feel rather lonely."

"Any time Edward goes to investigate a noise in the grounds or some movement about the house, I start to feel very afraid," Daisy added. "Since I was attacked, I find myself very anxious whenever I am alone."

"Quite understandable," Captain O'Harris said. "It was a horrible thing to happen. We intend to ensure nothing like that can occur again, while Clara is determined to find out who is the perpetrator."

"I am very grateful for that," Daisy nodded, then she regretted the movement as it caused a pain to shoot up her neck and across the back of her head. She reached up a hand to touch at her hair.

"Either Annie or Clara will be with you at all times," Captain O'Harris continued.

Daisy smiled at them, and her gaze fixed on to Annie.

"You're all very kind to come here and help me. I know this is not perhaps the usual sort of place you would expect to come, and I appreciate that things might seem a little odd around here for you. But I really do appreciate you taking the time to do this for me. If you have any questions about the Sun Club and how it operates, please do not hesitate to ask."

"Just so long as I don't have to see any naked people," Annie said sharply.

It was the first thing she had said to the group and her tone made O'Harris glance at her. He mentally winced at the way she had spoken.

Daisy did not react in the same way. She smiled at Annie; after all, she had experienced many people with similar attitudes.

"I can assure you of that Mrs Fitzgerald," she said calmly. "The rooms we are currently in are off limits to guests and can only be occupied if one is clad in clothes. This is what I consider the public side of the Sun Club, a place where visitors come. As long as you remain within these suites and the hallway that leads onto them, there should be no reason for you to see anyone unclad."

Annie was glad to hear that. She relaxed her shoulders a fraction and then, showing that she was conceding to the situation after all, she sat down on one of the sofas.

"It is going to be something of a long night," she said. "We ought to all get comfortable and prepare for what is ahead."

It was slightly impolite that Annie had sat down without being asked, and again O'Harris gave her that sideways look. It seemed that she was trying to take charge of the situation, but at least she was relaxing, so he did not criticise her openly.

Daisy waved her arm and indicated they should all be seated, and they settled themselves upon various pieces of furniture around the room.

"Oliver and I will be taking the first patrol around the gardens," Captain O'Harris explained. "We are going to keep as discreet a watch as possible. We want the intruder to get inside the grounds so we can capture them."

"I thought you were just going to scare them away?" Daisy responded, looking alarmed at this news.

"That is certainly one option, but if we want to know who is behind this and why, then we need to get hold of them. Scaring them away will only work for as long as we can be here. Better to find the culprits, don't you think?"

"He is quite right," Edward nodded. "We need to know who is behind this and why. I assume that Clara and Tommy have already ruled out the Reverend Lane as the culprit."

"Reverend Lane is denying all knowledge," O'Harris agreed. "In fact, he seems appalled at the news of what has happened. However, that does not rule out the possibility that someone in his protest group is responsible."

"People are truly extraordinary," Daisy shook her head sadly, once again regretting the movement and wincing in pain. She rubbed at her neck.

Annie's naturally caring nature came to the fore at that moment. She stood up and went over to Daisy and asked her politely to lean her head forward as much as she could. Daisy obeyed, and Annie took a good look at the bump on the back of her head.

"A cold compress might be useful," she said. "You have pain in your neck as well?"

"Yes, every time I move my head I feel a sharp pain in my neck. The doctor says I must have jerked my head forward when I was hit, and it has pulled the muscles. He says I must not move my head, but of course it's very difficult not to move your head when it's such an automatic thing to do."

"Some heat on your neck might help," Annie suggested. "We should warm up some cloths and rest them against the back of your neck, maybe we can then ease the muscles."

"Hot and cold. Quite the combination," Daisy managed to smile.

"You should also try to rest as much as possible," Annie continued. "And try not to worry about what is going on here."

"That is easier said than done when all things are considered," Daisy shrugged. "I have my guests to worry about after all."

"At this moment in time, we do not need to suppose there is any threat to your guests," O'Harris spoke. "The assault was on you, after all."

"You are failing to take into account what happened to poor Mr O'Brien," Daisy pointed out.

"That was an accident. There is no reason to suppose otherwise," O'Harris persisted.

Daisy almost nodded again, then she remembered herself and stopped just in time.

"Things have really become quite a mess in the last few days," she sighed. "What I wanted was to offer a place for the naturist movement. I wanted to offer somewhere people could be themselves. Instead, I've had all this drama. All this trouble. I have asked for none of it, and I have done my best to keep things as discreet as possible."

"Unfortunately, just the fact the Sun Club is here is enough to get some people worked up," O'Harris reminded her. "However, if you can survive this, I don't doubt that you will be able to continue here."

"Your confidence is reassuring," Daisy said to him. "But I don't really believe in it. Not at the moment, too much has happened. The rumours will go around, of course, and as soon as they do no one else will come."

"Try not to be so despondent," Edward told her placing a hand on her shoulder and lightly rubbing it. "We have to keep positive and hope for the best."

"Of course, I just feel like everything is falling apart all around me," Daisy leaned back on the sofa on which she was sitting. "I knew there were going to be protests. I knew someone would argue about why we're here. I did not think they would go so far as to wander on the grounds and strike at me. Then there is this bear business. I could hardly have anticipated that."

"No one could have anticipated the bear," O'Harris told her firmly.

"I had quite the job convincing my guests that they were in no danger here after what had occurred. They're still all somewhat shocked and have not been prepared to use the beach since the bear attack."

"Again, no one can blame you for what occurred out there," Edward reminded her. "It could have happened to anyone at any time."

Daisy seemed inclined to blame everything on herself, despite their words. Annie decided to take charge of her.

"We need to get your neck sorted first," she told her. "Then you must rest. We should worry about everything else after we have dealt with this situation. The evening is drawing on. It's getting dark. Captain O'Harris and Oliver ought to be getting out onto their patrol. Private Peterson and I will remain inside. Mr Wilton, what do you intend to do?"

Edward shrugged, rather thrown by her sudden dictatorial manner.

"Well, originally I was thinking of going upstairs and keeping an eye out the window for anything outside."

"Very sensible," Annie told him. "You can be our eyes and ears inside. You will see someone approaching the house and have an eagle eye view of everything. It is just a shame there is no way for you to communicate with Captain O'Harris and Oliver, so that you could send them to wherever they needed to go."

"We shall manage, as best we can," O'Harris smirked enjoying the fact that Annie was now completely involved in the situation and was even planning out how they were going to do things.

"Come on Oliver, it's time we got to work."

He and Oliver Banks left the room. Oliver had been quite quiet throughout the whole meeting, but he had been keeping an eye on the door leading to the hallway, and it was apparent he was hoping to catch a glimpse of the guests. It would be a good story to tell his journalist colleagues about how he had spent the night at the Sun Club. However, for the time being, no one was around. At least no one nude.

Peterson remained sitting politely on the sofa, waiting for instructions.

"First things first," Annie spoke up. "Let's find the kitchen. I want to know where everything is so I can make a cup of tea at any time that I wish. Now, Miss Belle, have you had any supper?"

"I didn't really..." Daisy began.

"Daisy has been struggling to eat with all the events that have been going on," Edward interjected.

"I don't seem to have any appetite," Daisy replied quietly. "And after the bang on the head, well, I've been feeling somewhat nauseous. To be honest, I have just been making do with the odd biscuit here and there."

"That will never do," Annie said sternly. "You need your strength up for whatever we've got to face. If the intruder is to come into the house and get past everybody, then me and you need to be at our very best to defeat them."

"You sound very confident about taking on somebody like that," Daisy said uneasily.

"I have dealt with intruders before," Annie said proudly. "Dare I say, they were far more dangerous intruders than whoever is liable to come into this house. The important thing is to keep your spirits up, and you can't do that on an empty stomach. Come on, Miss Belle, we're going to get you some food."

She offered the woman her arm and helped her to her feet. Daisy looked a bit disorientated by being suddenly taken under the wing of Annie, but she allowed herself to be walked away.

Private Peterson remained where he was sitting. He had not been told to do anything else, and he assumed that that was where he was needed. He would wait until he had further instructions. Edward glanced at him, received no particular response, and so headed upstairs leaving the ladies to whatever they intended to get up to.

It was going to be a strange night, that was for sure.

Chapter
Twenty-Four

Mr Drake gave the impression that he was avoiding Clara. Every time she decided she was going to confront him and ask him about his relationship with Daisy, he seemed to be in another part of the room, talking to someone else. When she inched over to try and infiltrate his conversation, he somehow managed to slip away from her or to act so engaged with the person he was currently talking to that it started to look awkward and impolite for her to remain standing nearby.

The more he made the effort not to talk to her, the more convinced Clara was she must talk to him at some point. The very fact he was avoiding her indicated that he had something to hide; that he had some reason to suspect why she was really there.

Could it be that Mr Drake had heard of the Fitzgeralds in connection to their private detective business? Or was it possible he had been paying closer attention to the Sun Club than anyone else realised? What if he had been watching the place and had seen Clara and Tommy enter? He would then be aware of their connection to

Daisy and also that they were unlikely to be true opponents of the Sun Club.

Whatever the reason, Clara had to talk to him. However, before she could get the opportunity, Reverend Lane brought the meeting to order, and they had to take a seat while he gave a short speech.

"I am delighted, as always, to see you all here," he said warmly. "It is always a pleasure to know I have so many like-minded friends."

This seemed slightly ingenuous considering the limited number of people present, which made it quite obvious that more people were either happy for the Sun Club to continue or were ambivalent about its presence.

"As you will all have noticed, we have two new members tonight. I am so pleased that other people from the area are taking an interest in this matter," Reverend Lane's announcement resulted in people turning their heads in Clara and Tommy's direction.

There was a smile on the face of Miss Soaper. Clara could not quite see the look on Mr Drake's face because he was being careful to keep just out of her eye line, but she could feel his gaze burning into her.

"I thought tonight it would be prudent to discuss our tactics going forward," Reverend Lane continued. "We have obviously made some big moves to try and get the Sun Club shut down. I have to commend Mrs Harper for her work in writing pieces for the local lady's magazine to try and drum up support. I am sure it is not due to lack of effort on her part that we have failed so far to see more of our genteel ladies coming along to join the group."

There was a general polite nodding of heads and approval of Mrs Harper's efforts.

"I personally have been speaking with the police, especially after the rather peculiar incident that happened on the beach below the Sun Club, and which, by now, you are all aware of. I have been assured that it had nothing directly to do with the Sun Club and was an unfortunate accident. However, I think we can all agree that such bizarre behaviour can only be the result of allowing immorality into this area. I would not go so far as to suggest it is God demonstrating his disapproval of the matter, but certainly I think the two things go hand in hand. Immorality and the resulting consequences."

"You get attacked by a bear if you're immoral?" Tommy whispered to his sister.

Clara shrugged.

"It would certainly solve a few problems."

"Unfortunately, at this moment in time the police have informed me they can do nothing for us. The Sun Club is not doing anything illegal."

There were groans from his fellow protest group attendees at this statement.

"I know, I know, but they are not doing anything against the law of the land. That is all I can say at the moment. In consequence we cannot rely on the police. I suggest we perhaps go back to protesting and raising awareness among other groups about Brighton. I am still writing to various bishops and the heads of the Church of England to get their attention to this matter in the hopes that they will put their weight behind this situation. In the meantime, I was thinking we could organise another small protest outside the gates - tomorrow morning perhaps? I believe we should be entitled to stay there for about an hour, any longer than that, and I fear the police might ask us to move on again."

There were soft murmurs of agreement. Surprising, really, Clara had assumed that there would be someone who raised the point that they had already tried protests without success, and maybe they needed to do something more dramatic. The ladies all seemed quite happy to put on another protest, talking about holding up placards and what they would bring in their lunch hampers to make the morning go by more pleasantly; it almost seemed as if they were organising a picnic.

Mr Plainer was silent. He folded his arms across his chest, and Clara got the impression that whatever occurred, he would not be part of it. He just wanted to keep track of what was happening with all this opposition to the Sun Club, but anything that involved actual action was not going to attract him. Mr Drake, who was sitting just next to him, using Plainer as a barrier between himself and the Fitzgeralds, was also silent on the subject.

"I'm glad to see we're all in agreement," Reverend Lane continued. "I want to take this opportunity to express clearly once again our manifesto, that we do not intend to do anything either violent or improper in nature to further our cause, that would be against what we all believe in. We are here to peacefully protest over this matter and to demonstrate that we are of the higher moral character in this regard. I know we're all in agreement, I just felt it was important I restate this as we now have some new members, and we need to be emphatic about what we intend to do."

Once more, curious gazes turned on Clara and Tommy.

"We shall do everything in our power to stop the Sun Club, but it shall be done in a proper and Christian fashion. If we fail in this regard and we cannot succeed, then we have to accept that that is the way God wishes things to be, and that some other force will come along to intercede on our behalf and achieve the desired effect."

"Do not speak in so defeatist a manner," Miss Soaper said loudly to the reverend. "We did not win the war by talking in such a manner."

"Quite right, Miss Soaper, and as long as I draw breath, I shall continue this battle. My point merely is that we have to accept this may take longer than we initially anticipated. I won't lie, I am somewhat disappointed that there is a lack of support among the local community for our protests."

"I am hardly surprised," Mrs Harper said coldly. "These days everyone is so heathen in their attitudes. Just look around at what is occurring. The ladies wear their skirts so short, and men barely have any manners these days."

"I blame it on the war," Miss Soaper agreed with her. "It changed everything for us. All those women taking up jobs in factories was utterly appalling. I believe that was the start of the rot."

"I worked in a factory during the war," Mrs Melton interjected quietly. "I found it a most productive use of my time and I felt very patriotic about it."

This aside soon had the ladies huddling in a group and discussing the matter further. Miss Soaper was endeavouring to retract her statement as she clearly was friendly with Mrs Melton, while Mrs Harper was protesting that any sort of work in a factory outside of the war was simply inappropriate.

Reverend Lane allowed this distraction for just a few moments and then tried to calm the ladies down. Clara had the impression this happened quite often.

"Back to the matter at hand, perhaps," he said politely. "While we all have our thoughts on what has caused us to reach this situation, what really matters is that we do all in our power to stop the Sun Club. We will go on a protest march tomorrow. It's going to be quite exciting."

Clara could not resist throwing oil on the water.

"It will be rather like the suffragette movement and how they did all those protests with their placards. Will we be chaining ourselves to the gates?"

Tommy nudged his sister hard in the ribs. Her introduction of the subject of the suffragettes had the desired effect, and the ladies went off on one once again. Mrs Melton was partly in favour of what they had done, while Miss Soaper was naturally against it, and Mrs Harper did not know where she stood. Miss Harper was very silent on the subject, and Clara got the impression she was a secret suffragette herself.

"Now, now, ladies, it will be nothing like the suffragette movement," Reverend Lane said, taking the time to cast a scowl in Clara's direction. She tried not to smile. "This will be a proper and polite sort of protest just as we have done before, and I told you it's perfectly acceptable."

"Quite right," Miss Soaper interjected. "These young women of today have no concept of how these things should be done."

She turned her own glare on Clara, who was now heartily amused.

"Can I just confirm with a show of hands who will be there to protest tomorrow?" Reverend Lane continued.

It was no surprise to anyone that the four hands that shot up were those of the ladies in the room, the two gentlemen kept their arms folded. Clara and Tommy, naturally, were not going to form part of the protest. Clara fancied they had already gained their answers about the ladies of this particular group. All she had now to do was to track down what was going on with Mr Plainer and Mr Drake.

"Will our newest members not be joining us?" Reverend Lane looked directly at the Fitzgeralds.

"Unfortunately, tomorrow is a work day," Clara told him.

This immediately set off the ladies again, who, while they could understand Tommy having a job, were alarmed to hear that Clara also worked. She was middle-class after all, and a middle-class lady did not have an occupation.

Clara was bombarded with questions about how she dared to have a job when she was clearly taking away work from a man. How could she be protesting the Sun Club when her own activities were somewhat immoral, at least to their minds. Even Mrs Melton joined in the barrage, as if she were trying to make up for the fact that she had worked in a factory during the war.

"My dear ladies, it's entirely up to the young Miss Fitzgerald if she has a job or not. None of you have actually asked her what she does. There are some quite respectable professions that women engage in and that none of us would argue about," Reverend Lane spoke up.

His clear voice dulled down the ire of the women, but Clara had no intention of explaining herself to them.

"What do you do then?" Mrs Harper asked her directly.

"I am not inclined to say," Clara told her with feigned affront. "After your reaction, I do not feel as though I wish to elaborate on my personal circumstances."

Clara had anticipated this would set the ladies off again. It took all of the Reverend Lane's powers of persuasion to get them to settle down once more.

"My, my look at the time, I think perhaps we ought to call an end to things," he said firmly. "I am delighted you could all make it, once again, and we shall see each other in the morning. I suggest we reconvene at eleven outside the gates of the Sun Club."

Briskly he brought the meeting to its conclusion. Clara was determined to now get a moment with Mr Drake. He, in turn, seemed to be in unseemly haste to get away from the meeting, confirming that he did not want to speak to them.

Making no goodbyes, he quickly grabbed up his hat and coat and was making for the door before anybody else. Even the ladies were distracted enough to note his sudden departure.

"Mr Drake, you seem to be in undue haste to leave us," Miss Soaper called out behind him.

Drake made the mistake of turning and looking back at her. In the brief moment it took for him to apologise for his departure speed, and to state that he had something he needed to attend to, Clara had also grabbed up her hat and coat and was hot on his heels.

She did not personally care if anybody thought she left with impolite haste. She had achieved what she needed from Reverend Lane and the ladies and did not anticipate she would be speaking to them again. The delay that Mr Drake had incurred meant that they caught up with him in the hallway.

He was just about out the door and looked at them with an expression of horror as he tried to make his departure.

"Better we speak to him outside," Clara whispered to her brother, who was quickly catching her up.

He nodded his agreement, and so they followed Mr Drake outside. He was hastening for the garden gate. Attempting to walk as fast as possible without actually breaking into a run. There was a bicycle propped up beside the wall and he was making for it. If he got on the bicycle, there was a good chance that he would elude them.

Tommy broke into a run, not himself worried about being seen jogging along the path and caught Mr Drake by the arm.

"Just a moment, Mr Drake," he said, smiling at him. "We haven't had a chance to talk."

"I have nothing I wish to say to either of you," Mr Drake said firmly, grabbing up the handlebars of his bicycle and trying to push it between himself and Tommy.

"I think we do have something to talk about," Clara said. "You have spent all evening avoiding us and I am now aware that you have a connection to Miss Belle at the Sun Club."

"That is a pure lie," Drake said quickly; the way his face paled indicated it was not.

"I very much doubt Mrs Soaper lied to me," Clara smiled at him. "She would not say something so radical without having some truth behind it. Besides which, the fact that you have avoided me all evening tells me more than her words."

"I haven't been avoiding anyone and I really need to get on. I have something to attend to."

"Might that be lurking in the grounds of the Sun Club to strike Miss Belle on the head again?" Tommy asked him darkly.

Drake was appalled by this information, and he stopped trying to push the bicycle into Tommy.

"What are you talking about?"

"Miss Belle was struck on the head by an intruder, and I think you're about the only person I've come across so far who had the motive to do something like that," Clara remarked. "Not to mention the inclination. It is quite plain to us that the protest group is peaceful, as it states."

"Mr Plainer clearly doesn't want to get his hands dirty, and is really just along for the ride," Tommy added. "You, however, you have a personal interest in this matter."

"I would never hurt Miss Belle," Drake protested.

"Then perhaps you better talk to us and explain exactly what has been going on," Clara replied to him. "Because, from where I stand, you are looking rather guilty."

Drake hung his head, realising the game was up. He groaned to himself.

"Very well, I will speak to you. But not here."

He was looking over their shoulder where the other members of the protest group were now leaving the house.

"I don't want anyone else knowing all my business."

"Come along, then," Tommy said. "Let's find somewhere quiet to have a little discussion."

Chapter
Twenty-Five

Mr Drake wheeled his bicycle along as they headed down the lane to a small area of trees where they could privately talk. The evening was dragging on now, the light slowly dimming and the last of the warmth disappearing. Clara pulled her coat tighter around her, trying to disappear into its cosy woollen fabric.

Mr Drake's own coat was rather thin. He looked cold and would have probably appreciated being home by his own warm fire. They finally found a spot among the shadows of some trees where they would not be easily noticed, far enough away from Reverend Lane's house that none of the other guests would come upon them and hear what they were to say.

"In some regards, I am glad you caught me up and asked me about this," Drake said, once they had stopped. He had propped his bicycle against a tree, and was now leaning back on another one, hands in his pockets. "I feel like it's been a terrible secret hanging over me."

"Then it is true that you were engaged to Miss Belle?" Clara asked him.

"Completely true," Drake agreed. "We were engaged for a full year, then Daisy called it off. When I think about it, I don't suppose we were ever a true match. I felt for her more than she ever felt for me. Even so, it was something of a shock when she left me and took up with that Edward Wilton."

"You know about him then?" Tommy spoke.

"I could hardly not know about him," Drake shrugged. "Not long after we had broken off the engagement, I saw her walking out with him. My suspicion is that she was already inclined towards him before we separated and that was the reason for calling off our wedding."

"Better she did that before you were wed than after, old boy," Tommy told him.

"No doubt you are correct. But it still stung."

"Is that why you wish to see the Sun Club fail?" Clara asked him.

"I don't want to see it fail precisely," Drake looked uneasy. "That is not the way I would phrase things. What I want is for Daisy to realise what she is doing. To see that she is making such a mess of things. That her reputation is at risk. I want her to realise that she should be doing something else with her life, and I don't mean getting back with me because I appreciate that is not going to happen. I just want her to see some sense."

"But it is not up to you," Tommy reminded him. "She is entitled to do exactly as she pleases."

"I still feel for her though, don't I?" Drake countered. "I want her to be happy, of course I do. And if to be happy it means she has to be with Edward Wilton, then so be it. But I can't see how she can be happy if she is making such a fool of herself and turning people so against her."

Clara was not convinced by his protests. She did not believe his upset was purely about the fact that he still cared for Daisy. She sensed there was an element of revenge going on. Perhaps he didn't think it was revenge against Daisy herself, but rather against Edward, but it was there, nonetheless.

"If the Sun Club fails, Daisy will lose an awful lot," she reminded him. "I have no doubt she has invested a lot of money in getting the business up and running. She might even lose her home over it."

"I'm sure that would not be the case. Why couldn't she just run a respectable sort of institution instead, a nice hotel, for instance, out in the countryside or one of those retirement homes for elderly gentlemen?"

"And that would be a better use for the Sun Club?" Tommy raised an eyebrow at him. "Can you really imagine Daisy running a retirement home?"

Drake shook his head.

"My point is that she needs to stop all this nonsense."

"How far would you go to get her to stop?" Clara asked him next.

"Not as far as you are suggesting," Drake scowled at her and, for once, there was real venom in his voice. She saw another side to him. He could get angry when he wanted to defend himself.

"Daisy was attacked on her own grounds," Clara persisted. "Someone climbed over the wall and when they saw her in the woods they attacked her. It could be that they were merely surprised by her presence and wanted to get away, or it could be that they wanted to cause her harm, to scare her perhaps, to make her think twice about what she was doing."

"I would never do something like that," Drake insisted. "I care for Daisy. I always have. I just want what's best for her."

"But your peaceful protest is not achieving anything," Tommy reminded him. "Maybe you thought you needed to press your point home."

"You can try and insinuate that I have done something wrong, and I will keep insisting I have not, and you have no proof of anything. You can ask Daisy and she will tell you that I have always been a perfect gentleman."

"Don't doubt we will speak to her about this matter," Clara promised him.

Drake suddenly frowned.

"I didn't mean for you to actually speak to her. Don't tell her I've been doing this. I've been avoiding being seen; not attending the protests or anything, so she won't know. I don't want her to know that I am behind this."

"You just wanted to secretly destroy her life," Tommy told him coldly.

"You are wrong about that. It's not about destroying her life; it's about salvaging it."

"I think Daisy would see things very differently," Clara told him sternly. "Now I have one last question for you. Where were you last night?"

"Where was I?" Drake looked at them in confusion. "I was at home, of course. Where else would I be?"

"Do you live alone?" Tommy asked him.

"I do, unless you count my cat. Are you trying to determine whether I was out here stalking Daisy last night?"

"Well, it would have been useful if you had an alibi for the time of the attack," Clara told him. "You didn't speak to anybody, maybe a neighbour? Or do anything that could have been seen by someone?"

"I don't think so. I am something of a quiet person. Once I'm at home, I am not inclined to speak to people or go out again. That was always one of the things that Daisy protested about. She's always been rather sociable."

"It strikes me you were rather chalk and cheese," Tommy remarked.

"Perhaps we were. But I thought that made us all the better together. She shouldn't have left me for him, you know."

"But she did, and now you have to move on," Tommy informed him. "You need to forget all about her. She will not thank you for what you are doing, and you are just making things worse. Go home, forget all about the Sun Club and never returned to Reverend Lane's meetings."

"You cannot tell me what to do," Drake snapped back.

"No, but I can advise you and that is my advice. It is time you moved on from this."

Drake made a snorting noise, but he said no more on the subject.

"Are you quite finished with me?"

"You can go," Clara said, moving away.

He grabbed up his bicycle and pushed it towards them, skimming Clara's dress with the wheel. She had no doubt he had managed to get some oil onto it. Looking disgruntled, Drake mounted the bicycle and sauntered off, wobbling for a few paces before he got into his stride.

"What do you think?" Tommy asked when he was far enough away not to overhear them.

"Personally, I still think he could have done it," Clara replied. "He has no alibi, and he is very angry about the situation with Daisy. He is just the sort of fellow with that quiet, simmering nature to suddenly react angrily and violently."

"We can't prove anything," Tommy reminded her. "All we have is suspicion."

"Well, if it was him, hopefully we scared him away enough that he won't try anything again," Clara added. "In the meantime, we just keep exploring things. It won't hurt to speak to Daisy and ask her what she thinks of the likelihood that he attacked her."

"It would certainly make more sense of why the attack was from behind. We said that the person probably did not want to be seen. Drake would not want Daisy seeing his face and recognising him."

"We failed to ask him how he happened to know who we were," Clara said, sighing that they had overlooked this. "That might have given us some sort of idea. If he's been lurking around the Sun Club, that is how he could have seen us there."

"He would have lied about that, too." Tommy consoled her. "We just have to keep soldiering on to figure this out."

They were already walking back down the lane, heading on the long route towards the Sun Club.

"I wonder how everyone else is getting on tonight," Clara remarked as they wandered.

"I imagine it has been very quiet," Tommy assured her. "Whatever has been going on, I suspect it is all going to blow over now."

"You sound very confident about that."

"I *am* very confident. I have a good feeling about the way things are going. I think everything is going to be all right now."

Annie had dozed off in the comfortable armchair that sat next to the fire in the sitting room where she, Peterson, and Daisy were spending the evening. It was getting late. Annie was usually in bed by this time, and she was starting to feel the fatigue of the day, as she always did. Annie could never be described as being anything but excessively busy, and by the evenings she was always exhausted and looking forward to a good night's rest.

She had done her best to make Daisy more comfortable – cold

compresses to the back of her head, warm cloths to the back of her neck – and the lady did say that she was feeling better. She too was resting on the sofa and close to dozing off.

Peterson was the one who remained alert. Not just because he felt it was his place to watch over them, but because he very rarely slept well. He suffered nightmares that made it easier to avoid shutting his eyes than it did to fall asleep.

He was currently stationed by the window that looked out over the lawn. Evening had drawn on properly so he could only see a fraction outside, the cosy glow of the fire making it difficult to see further. Still, he might pick up some movement if anything occurred.

There was no sign as yet of Clara and Tommy. Annie was not terribly concerned about that. She knew how far it was to the meeting and that it would take a while for them to walk back. They were together, and that made her feel better. As long as they were together, how much trouble could they get into?

There had been no news either from Edward. Daisy had remarked a while ago that it was entirely possible he had fallen asleep. Everything, in fact, was rather quiet. It seemed as if they were in for a peaceful night.

Annie was roused from her light doze by rapping on the door. Peterson swung around on his heel as if he were on a military parade. Daisy jerked from her own repose and lifted her head slowly.

"Who is there?" Annie called out.

A tentative voice spoke from behind the door.

"It is Mrs Geneva. Might I speak to Miss Belle if she is in there?"

Daisy was now sitting up on the sofa.

"Come in, Mrs Geneva."

The door opened and in came a rotund woman wearing a garish floral dress. The patterns were large and boisterous on the fabric, and only seemed to enhance the woman's rather large bosom. She had to be in her fifties and Annie was surprised to see someone of her age and size attending a club where one spent a lot of one's time without their clothes on.

"I am sorry to disturb you this evening," Mrs Geneva spoke. "I don't suppose either of you have seen Mr Geneva?"

Annie had been forewarned that everyone in the club used pseudonyms, so she assumed that 'Mrs Geneva' was not the lady's real name.

"Your husband is missing?" Daisy stood up.

"Not precisely missing," Mrs Geneva said. "He went out for a walk this evening and he has not returned. I was expecting him back at least half an hour ago. I wouldn't have worried, of course, except for the fact of everything that's been going on."

"I remember I specifically asked all the guests not to go out after dark," Daisy said and there was a sharp edge to her tone.

"My husband always goes for a walk in the evening. He can't sleep otherwise," Mrs Geneva countered. "And he is not afraid of any bear."

"I should go out and look for him," Private Peterson declared. "I shall signal for Captain O'Harris and Oliver so that we can look together."

This seemed the only feasible thing to do.

"Mrs Geneva, do you know where your husband went?" Annie asked her.

"He always walks in the direction of the beach," Mrs Geneva replied. "He likes the sea air and to hear the waves."

"I shall head in that direction," Peterson told them, and he departed the room, politely bowing to Mrs Geneva. She was too flustered by everything to really notice his manners but moved out of the way to let him through the door.

Daisy did not seem to know quite how to handle the situation after that, so Annie took charge. She could see that Mrs Geneva was more worried than she was letting on.

"I suggest you come and sit down over here," she told her. "We will make you a cup of tea."

"Thank you," Mrs Geneva said. "I didn't like to interrupt you. I know these rooms are technically off limits to the guests. But I was getting so worried about everything."

"Not to worry," Daisy told her. "You were quite right to come and see us, sit down at once."

They settled the woman in a chair and went about the procedure of making a fresh pot of tea. By the time they had served it along with several biscuits, another half hour had slipped by and there was no sign of Peterson or anyone else.

Annie was trying not to look at the clock, but she couldn't help but think to herself that the woman before her must be doing the same. Mrs Geneva must be counting down the minutes, and with each one that passed, she would be even more inclined to think something serious had happened to her husband.

"I did tell him he shouldn't go for a walk," she said quietly after they had drunk tea for a while. "I reminded him of what you had said, Miss Belle. But he was insistent. He doesn't sleep well at all, you know. He says that if he doesn't have a walk, then he stands no chance of getting off to sleep."

"That is perfectly understandable," Daisy said, though the edge to her tone suggested she did not understand it at all. She was worried as well. That was making everyone tense.

"He will turn up, of course," Mrs Geneva said, trying to smile. "I'm sure he just got a bit lost in the dark. The grounds are somewhat indistinct and there are all those woods."

Annie was also thinking there was the cliff edge and that sharp fall down onto the beach that Mr Hercules had come across unexpectedly. What if Mr Geneva had done something similar, walked a little too far, lost his way in the dark, and stumbled?

"I'm sure we shall have this all resolved very soon," Daisy reassured Mrs Geneva.

She was just about to offer her another cup of tea when there was a movement by the door. Both her and Annie glanced up. Mrs Geneva started to her feet, expecting to see her husband. Instead, the person who appeared at the doorway was Private Peterson. The look on his face told them that the news was not good.

Chapter Twenty-Six

The autumn evening had turned cold as Clara and Tommy worked their way back to the Sun Club. The roads were unlit, so they were having to make their way as best they could using the insubstantial beam of Tommy's torch. The gates were up ahead, and Clara was surprised to see that one of them was stood slightly open. She was even more surprised to note that there was someone waiting for them there. She assumed it was the gatekeeper who had been told of their arrival at some point and was waiting to greet them. She was not expecting to see Captain O'Harris.

"At last you two are here," he said, striding out of the gates before they reached them.

There was a look of deep concern on his face. Clara knew that look. Something terrible had happened. She rushed the last few steps towards him and caught him by the hand.

"What has happened, John?"

"Another death, Clara," O'Harris said without preamble. "Another guest. He goes by the name of Mr Geneva, and he went for a walk earlier this evening. When he didn't come back, we went looking for him. We found him all right."

"I thought Daisy was going to tell everybody to stay in the house once it started to get dark," Tommy said.

"And so she did," O'Harris agreed. "Mr Geneva chose not to listen to that instruction. Apparently he always has an evening walk and no talk of bears or anything else would have deterred him."

"I can't believe the intruder has taken this next step," Clara shook her head. "I had not anticipated that they would go so far in their efforts to be rid of the Sun Club."

"We don't know precisely if it was an intruder," O'Harris pointed out, revealing in his face that there was more to this matter than met the eye. "The victim appears to have claw marks across their chest, just like our previous victim."

"Claw marks?" Tommy could not believe what he was hearing.

"Precisely," O'Harris nodded. "It would seem that we've had another bear attack."

"That is preposterous," Clara said, alarmed by this development. "I could almost understand the first attack, but this second one? Why would the bear attack another grown man?"

"Maybe it is rabid?" Tommy suggested. "Perhaps that is why someone allowed it to escape their private zoo."

"I cannot believe anyone would be so irresponsible as to allow a rabid bear to roam the countryside."

"You would be surprised how callous people can be," Tommy shrugged. "Anyway, it's just a suggestion, though it is curious that it has attacked twice here, and yet in neither instance has it eaten anyone. At least, I'm assuming that our latest victim was not eaten?"

"No, you are quite right. Apart from the claw marks, the man was untouched by an animal," O'Harris confirmed. "Perhaps you better come see for yourselves."

He led them across the lawn leaving behind the gatekeeper to close the gates, the man then went and huddled in his little hut. Clara imagined that he was intending to make sure the door was bolted closed if he could. They walked towards the house, which was cast in darkness. There was just one light that glowed out of a side window leaving a patch of yellow on the lawn beside it. O'Harris veered around the house, taking them around to the back, pointing across the gardens. They didn't have to go far to find the man. He was lying on the tennis courts.

They were in time to see the arrival of Peterson, Daisy, and Annie. Peterson was relieved to see O'Harris had found Clara and Tommy.

"Before we all crowd around this body," Clara said, stepping in front of Daisy deliberately, "Someone needs to go back inside and telephone the police."

"Oh, Clara, not again," Daisy groaned.

"I am afraid so. The sooner they are summoned, the better, and with it being dark, at least no one will be able to see much of what is going on."

"I'll go," Annie volunteered, walking back to the house.

As she strode back, she passed a woman heading towards them. Out of the corner of her eye, Clara became aware of this new person. She was an older woman, robust in appearance, moving in a slow fashion that suggested she was hoping not to get too close to the scene of the death. Clara turned her attention in the woman's direction.

"Who is that?"

Daisy turned her head and glanced back the way they had just come.

"Oh, that is Mrs Geneva. I told her to remain in the sitting room. I guess she decided to follow us after all."

"Peterson, go keep an eye on that woman," O'Harris nodded to the private. "I don't want her getting too close to her husband's body."

Peterson signalled his understanding and hastened back up the path where he stopped beside Mrs Geneva and offered her his arm. She took it and leaned on him heavily, seeming about to collapse, and grateful for his assistance. He kept her just a short distance away from the rest of them, talking to her.

"He is rather good at looking after other people," Tommy remarked to O'Harris. "A natural, I would say."

"Well, you know what they say, when you've had experience of bad things yourself, you're better at helping others going through the same. He is very good with people who are in distress. I've seen it when new fellows have come to the Home. Peterson is usually the first one to reach out to them."

Clara was only half listening to this discussion. She was leading the march towards the body. She wanted to be the first to see what was going on.

"Tommy I will need your torchlight over here."

Tommy hurried to be at her side and cast the flimsy beam onto a huddled shape on the tennis court. Mr Geneva had not been a particularly handsome fellow in life. In death, his hooked nose, protruding jaw, and sallow appearance was only enhanced. He lay fallen on his back, his legs hitched up and twisted to the right, his arms splayed out on either side. His eyes were still open, and there was a look of horror upon his face, though Clara was aware that this could mean nothing. Anything could happen when a body was in its death throes, and she had learned that it was best not to judge how horrific a person's death was by the appearance on their face. She had heard people talk of someone being scared to death, basing this on an expression on the features, but she knew full well that was not something that truly occurred. There was always something else behind someone's death.

Clara crouched by the body to take a better look. Tommy's torch only lit up sections of it. He started at the head and slowly moved the beam downward until Clara asked him to stop. It had fallen on the claw marks across the man's chest.

"Four of them," she said to Tommy. "Just like before and as if an animal has scratched its claws across him like this."

She demonstrated her idea by moving her arm across the body, her hand above the wounds so she didn't interfere with it.

"Then we do have the work of a bear again," Tommy said.

"You remember what Dr Deáth said before. He could not be certain exactly what made these claw marks. I also find it very curious that this man was killed but not eaten. Bears do not just randomly attack people for no reason."

"Maybe the bear felt it needed protect itself," Tommy suggested.

"And what was a bear doing wandering around the tennis courts?" Clara raised an eyebrow at him. "It's not as though these are a logical place for it to be. Far too close to human habitation. The beach I could almost understand. This doesn't seem right."

"You are forgetting it came from a private collection and is probably quite used to people. Maybe it came here to look for food."

"In which case, that denies your argument that it was scared. A bear that is used to people is more likely to approach them than it is to attack them."

"That does seem to be something of a conundrum," Tommy agreed.

"Also, these wounds are not that deep. I can't see how they would have killed him."

Tommy now crouched down beside her and drew the torchlight even closer to the corpse. He examined the claw marks for a moment or two.

"You are right. They are shallow, certainly not something that would kill a man."

"Yet we have a lot of blood scattering across the tennis court," Clara pointed out. "It has to have come from somewhere, and by the looks of it, and the way it's spread, I would say it was a wound that spurted blood rather than leaked it."

Tommy was now carefully letting the light play across the wounds themselves.

"There is a deeper wound just here on the edge of this claw mark," he observed. "By the position I would suggest the wound goes straight into the heart."

"Such a wound as that would certainly spurt blood when the offending weapon was drawn out again," Clara agreed. "But that is not the sort of wound a claw would make. It would imply that the bear somehow stabbed the man with one single claw deep enough to enter the heart, and that is inconsistent with the slash marks."

"Then could the slash marks be hiding the stab wound?" Tommy suggested. "Look how they have been positioned to cover that particular injury."

"If that is the case, then what we are looking at is deliberate murder and someone trying to mask it as the work of a bear. And that leads us to the ominous conclusion that Mr Hercules did not die by accident either."

"Perhaps one of the protest group decided that they were going to destroy the Sun Club by murdering its guests."

"That is quite an extreme way to go about things," Clara remarked. "I'm not convinced that anybody we met tonight would be that way inclined."

"What about Mr Drake? He rode off in the direction of the Sun Club. He could have easily reached here well ahead of us and committed this crime."

"I suppose it is a possibility. He did not strike me as someone who would go around carrying a knife ready to murder someone. But then, do we really know what a person is like, just from one conversation?"

"And he clearly is very upset about the fact Daisy is running this place," Tommy reminded her. "I think we have to go with the possibility that he did do this. Though it was brazen to commit this act only moments after he had spoken to us and denied the fact that he had done anything here."

"If he did do this after what he said to us, then he is a very disturbed and dangerous man indeed. But if he didn't do this, then I'm really not sure who we can supply as a suspect."

Clara rose from the ground. She had seen all she really needed to from Mr Geneva. Unlike the previous victim, he was fully clothed. The shirt he had been wearing had been ripped open by the claws. Clara gave him one last look and then looked around at the scene of the crime.

"It might be worth our while to take a look around the bushes that are either side of the tennis court to see if we can spot a knife," she said to Tommy. "Though I very much expect the killer has taken it with them like they did the first time."

"Tossing away a knife would be extra proof that it wasn't a bear attack, and quite clearly that is not what the person wishes people to imagine. He wants to mask the fact that he is committing murder."

"That is true. But from whom is he most worried about hiding that fact? The police and the general public? Or from those who might know why he would be attacking the victims and might suspect him?"

"Why not both?" Tommy replied.

Clara shrugged.

"Yes, why not?"

From behind them, they heard the uneven voice of Daisy. She was trying to control her emotions as she spoke. Edward had caught up with her now, having been summoned by Captain O'Harris and he had his arm around her, trying to console her.

"Is he dead?" Daisy asked. "You are absolutely certain of it?"

Clara returned to her and placed a hand on her arm.

"I'm sorry to say he *is* dead," she explained.

"Another bear attack?" Daisy shook her head, unable to take in the information. "How is it possible that this happened to me, to us, to poor Mr Geneva? All he did was go for a little walk."

"It was not just a bear attack," Clara told her. "But really, we need to wait for the police before we discuss this any further. We must make sure that all the other guests are safe and inside, and I think I better talk to Mrs Geneva."

Clara was glancing behind Daisy towards the older woman, who was still being consoled by Peterson. Though she seemed troubled by what had occurred, she was bearing up surprisingly well under the circumstances. She had not insisted on being allowed to see her husband which Clara thought was odd. In most situations, a devoted wife would insist on coming to see where their fallen spouse was lying. Instead, Mrs Geneva seemed quite content to just lean on Peterson and observe what was happening from a distance.

"We should get everybody inside and wait for the police to arrive," Clara repeated herself.

"There was one other thing, Clara," O'Harris said from behind them. She turned in his direction. "I appear to have misplaced Oliver."

"Oliver has disappeared?" Clara said in alarm.

"We were doing a sweep of the grounds together and then his torch started to fail. He said he was going to go back to the house and grab some new batteries, so I carried on. It was at that moment, as I came across the lawn that I spied something on the tennis court and came over to take a look. In the commotion that occurred afterwards I forgot all about Oliver. But he seems to have, well, vanished."

They all looked around them in some alarm.

"He can't have gone far," Tommy said, trying to console himself about the fact that he had forgotten about Oliver too. "You know what Oliver is like. He's probably lost."

"Whatever the case, we need to find him as soon as possible," Clara added. "We should get everybody who isn't needed for the search back into the house, and then we better take a good look around for him. Who knows what trouble Oliver could have got himself into while he's been left to his own devices."

Chapter
Twenty-Seven

Tommy, Clara, O'Harris, Peterson, and Edward all spread out to go in search of Oliver. O'Harris indicated where he had last seen him as he was on his way to the house. They fanned out from there, hoping to find him sooner rather than later. Clara was troubled that she had agreed to allow Oliver onto their little mission. It had evened up the numbers, but she had to admit Oliver was prone to getting himself into trouble. At the time, she had not thought there was anything he could particularly do wrong. After all, they were only trying to deter or capture an intruder and not one she had anticipated would be so violent. Other than the assault on Daisy, the intruder seemed to be more inclined to keep out of the way. Now they had this second attack, she was beginning to doubt her own assessment. What if the man was a lunatic, striking out at people randomly? Then again was a lunatic rational enough to mask what he was doing by pretending a bear had attacked someone?

They spread out in a line, each within calling distance of another so that no one else would accidentally go missing and they spread out across the grounds. They decided to go towards the east of the house as that was where O'Harris had last seen Oliver and he had not seen anyone go past him when he was on the tennis courts. It seemed logical that if Oliver had been snatched by anyone, it would have been on the east side of the house. It was also the direction in which the woods were. If anyone was going to keep Oliver a prisoner or do something nefarious to him, they were going to do it in the cover of the woods.

Of course, there was no knowing quite what trouble Oliver might have got himself into without outside assistance while he was seemingly just getting batteries. Oliver being Oliver, it was entirely possible that he had come up with some notion about searching the woods by himself, had disappeared off alone and was now hopelessly lost among the trees. Whatever the case, Clara was deeply regretting getting him involved. They had enough problems on their hands without worrying about what had become of him.

All he had to do was go back to the house.

O'Harris had told her that they had not been far away from it at the time they parted. Literally within spitting distance. So how on earth could he have simply disappeared?

Clara felt awful. She was the one who had involved him and now she felt guilty about the possibility he had been hurt. They called out Oliver's name, thinking that if someone had got hold of him, it might spook them into letting him go. They were halfway across the lawn when they heard someone shouting out in reply.

"Over here."

With relief, Clara realised the voice she could hear was that of Oliver. She darted forward, even though O'Harris shouted out that they were to keep in line. She could not resist. She needed to find him and if someone was holding him and using him to lure her into a trap, well, heaven help them because they were about to have her fury descend upon them.

Tommy was hot on her heels, as were the other men. She darted through the woods, shouting for Oliver to keep calling so she could locate him. The woods were not deep or dense, yet there were enough trees that in the darkness it was easy to become disorientated and to find yourself not knowing where you were going.

Oliver continued to call out. He sounded quite chipper, not as if he were being held hostage by someone with a knife to his neck. In fact, he sounded positively enthusiastic. This encouraged Clara, and so she stumbled forward, tripping over loose branches and tree roots, occasionally snagging her clothes on some rampant brambles.

She came out of the little patch of woods she was in, into a sort of clearing. It wasn't much of an open space, just a slightly wider area between the trees, and there she saw Oliver. On the ground before him, kneeling, was Mr Drake. She was so taken by surprise at this scene that she came to a sharp stop. So sharp that Tommy, who had been just behind her, bounced into her as he came through the trees and nearly knocked her sprawling. He grabbed her arm in time to steady her, and then they both stood, staring at Oliver.

"I have caught the intruder," Oliver said in a cheery voice, excited by what he had been up to.

Now they looked closer, they could see that Mr Drake was not just kneeling, but had his hands tied behind his back. Where Oliver had come across a piece of cord to achieve this feat, they did not know.

Oliver was quite delighted to see them.

"I was going back to the house for some batteries for my torch, when I heard someone moving in the bushes and then I saw this fellow running across the lawn. I chased him. I know I should have called for Captain O'Harris, but I was flushed with the heat of the moment and the pursuit. It was like being a hound after the fox," Oliver was smiling broadly at his triumph. "I chased the man right into these woods. There was just enough light from my dwindling torch to pursue him among the trees, and then I caught him. I couldn't believe it. I got him and I tied him up. Then I thought I best wait for someone to come find me. I knew you would all look for me once I failed to turn up."

"Where did you get the rope from?" Tommy asked him.

"Oh, I brought that with me. Just in case we had to tie up a suspect. Never thought I would get to use it."

O'Harris, Peterson, and Edward had now appeared on the scene. O'Harris was taking in everything, his sharp eyes noting, as Clara had done, that this was not an obvious situation for Oliver to be in. It was far more usual for him to be the one kneeling on the ground with his hands tied behind his back.

"Precisely how did you catch him?" O'Harris questioned.

Oliver's smile twitched a little.

"Well, you know, I'm a pretty good sprinter," he said.

"I tripped," Mr Drake said bluntly from the ground. "Right over that big root there and went face down. He wouldn't have caught me otherwise."

Oliver flinched. Clara was sympathetic.

"Don't worry Oliver, it is perfectly all right. After all, if he had a good head start you would have had no hope of catching him up. You had the quick thinking to tie him up and that's all that matters."

"Precisely," Oliver said, his smile returning. "I should say this is the fellow that's been causing us all that bother. Here we are. Case solved."

He stared around them wondering why they were not all looking relieved and delighted with him.

"Did he happen to have a knife on him," O'Harris asked.

Not only did Oliver start at this question, but Mr Drake raised his head sharply too.

"What are you suggesting? I would never carry a knife."

"Then what were you doing here on the grounds after we had just had that conversation with you about the fact that you were *not* the intruder and had *not* assaulted Miss Belle?" Clara demanded sarcastically.

"Wait, this is the fellow that attacked Daisy?" Edward stepped forward, his fists clenched and looking as if he were about to give Drake a pounding.

O'Harris caught him by the arm and pulled him back.

"We don't know that just yet, Edward," he reminded him.

"Why you are here, Mr Drake?" Clara persisted.

Mr Drake ducked his head, no longer able to meet them in the eye.

"I wasn't intending any harm," he said. "I thought after you had said to me what had happened here and how upset Daisy was... Well, you never know, she might have needed consoling, and I was going to be the one to do that consoling."

"Funny way to go about things," Tommy barked. "You hit her over the head the last time you were here, and then when you've scared her sufficiently, you act as if you're the big hero, coming to make sure if she's all right."

"If that was the case, how come you were lurking in the bushes?" Oliver said.

"A very good point," Clara remarked. "Seems to me that our Mr Drake has a lot of explaining to do."

"All right, all right," Drake said, ducking his head further. He was a coward deep down at heart, only prepared to strike out when he was hidden in the shadows and now with all of them glaring at him, he was finding it difficult to maintain his composure. "So maybe I came to see what was happening here. See if I could stir things up a bit more."

"Then you *were* the man who came into the grounds and assaulted

Daisy the other night," Clara had her arms folded across her chest, and she was glaring at him hard.

Drake swallowed. He glanced around them, his eyes falling on Edward, who looked about ready to beat him into a pulp.

"I want you to promise you will protect me from him," he said, nudging his head in the direction of Edward. "He looks like he wants my blood."

"If you make a full confession of what you are doing here," Clara said. "Then I will ensure your safety. You will have to answer for your crimes, you know, Mr Drake and the police are on their way."

Drake looked alarmed by this information.

"But it was only a spot of trespassing, and I didn't really intend to hurt Daisy. She surprised me, you see, and I couldn't have her seeing me here. I didn't really mean to hit her that hard. I just flailed out with a stick I had in my hand. Then, when she went down, I was so panicked that I dashed for the wall."

"How heroic," Edward glared at him his words cold. "You struck her and then just left her there."

"But I couldn't let her see me," Drake continued trying to explain himself. "She couldn't know it was me who had been looking around the grounds. All I wanted to do was get some information that I could take to the press or the police to prove the Sun Club was doing something illegal. Then I could get the place shut down."

"You are saying you had no intentions of harming anyone?" Clara asked carefully.

"No, no, nothing like that. I'm not a violent man. I admit what happened with Daisy perhaps gives that impression, but that was out of sheer panic. I was merely trying to find some way of getting back into Daisy's affections."

Edward startled at this information.

"What do you mean by that?"

Clara answered on the behalf of Drake.

"Mr Drake and Daisy were once engaged," she told Edward. "Quite sensibly, Daisy called the whole thing off."

"You were trying to cause the Sun Club so much trouble that Daisy would fail in her business and, what, she'd come running back to you?" Tommy said.

Drake grimaced.

"I had my hopes," he said. "I mean, I didn't think he," he nodded his head in the direction of Edward, "would be any use in a crisis. I would have taken her back, supported her. Made her feel better."

"But you were going to destroy her in the first place," Clara told him coldly. "That is not the act of someone who cares about someone else. Tell me, when did this matter take a darker turn for you?"

"What do you mean?" Drake said, looking suspiciously at her.

"When did you decide to murder people?"

It was not just Drake who flinched at her words. Oliver looked amazed and startled.

"What happened when I wasn't there?" He said, glancing towards O'Harris.

"Someone else has been stabbed," O'Harris told him bluntly. "And it looks like Mr Drake here is the one responsible."

"What? No, no, no. I would never do anything like that," Drake insisted. "I was only here to observe, to see something that I could report to the police. I have never hurt anyone."

"You keep saying that and you keep forgetting that you struck Daisy," Tommy told him fiercely. "That means you are a liar."

Drake shook his head even more vigorously.

"That was an accident. I wouldn't ever set out to hurt someone deliberately, and I haven't killed anyone. I didn't even know there was another body. Honestly, I would never do anything like that." "We should search him for a knife," O'Harris said.

Without being asked, Peterson stepped forward and roughly searched Mr Drake, looking in his coat jacket, searching his pockets, even feeling around his waistband to see if he had a knife pushed down his belt. He turned back to them.

"He's unarmed."

"I told you," Drake insisted. "I would never hurt anybody."

They were ignoring him now, along with his denials.

"We best take him back to the house and keep him secure for the police to question. He's probably thrown the knife away," Clara said, then she looked a bit closer at Drake. "It's hard to tell in the dark, however, he does not appear to have any blood splatter on him. That wound that Mr Geneva had would almost certainly have cast blood on the murderer."

Tommy took out his torch and flashed it across Drake's jacket and shirt. It was a white shirt and as far as he could tell, it was pristine. The jacket was brown, which made it harder to say if there were any stains upon it. It would be easier to know when they were inside under the glare of artificial light.

"I am telling you, I have never hurt anybody in my life... apart from Daisy. What I mean is, I wouldn't do this sort of thing. I would never stab someone or cause someone to die. Such a horrible thought. I didn't even serve in the war, you know. I was a pacifist."

All these ramblings were not assisting him. They were just increasing their irritation at his presence; remarking that he was a pacifist when he was surrounded by four men who had served and suffered in the war hardly endeared him to them.

"Get him to his feet, Oliver, let's get him back to the house," O'Harris said sternly.

Oliver was only too happy to obey. He yanked Mr Drake to his feet and pushed him a little to send him in the right direction.

"Well done, Oliver, on your quick thinking," Clara said, recalling that no one had praised Oliver for what he had achieved. "You may very well have just caught a murderer. Your first, I might add."

Oliver beamed with pride and stood up a little taller.

"Tell me the truth, Clara, when you realised I wasn't at the house and you wondered where I was, you were thinking that I had ended up stabbed by the murderer, didn't you?"

Tommy suddenly coughed to mask the laugh that was threatening to spill out of his mouth. Clara pursed her lips, trying to suppress her own discomfort.

"It might have crossed my mind," she admitted. "Though I gave you the benefit of the doubt."

Oliver laughed heartily.

"Of course you did, and that's why you are all out here searching for me. You thought I'd got myself into trouble again."

"Well, old man, it wouldn't be the first time," Tommy smirked.

Oliver, rather than being offended, was heartily amused by this, and kept chuckling all the way back to the house as he carefully pushed and guided Drake to keep walking in the right direction.

Chapter
Twenty-Eight

Daisy was waiting for them at the door to the kitchen of the house. When she saw them approaching, she stepped forward. The first person she recognised was Drake and her mouth fell open.

"What is he doing here?" She demanded, her tone so angry and fierce that Clara wondered that Drake had ever supposed he could win her back.

Edward rushed towards her. He still wanted to pound his fists into Drake, and he was getting testy about being held back. Now he stood by Daisy and clutched her hand in his.

"This is the man who struck you, Daisy," he said.

Daisy pressed her lips together.

"I never wanted to see you again, Victor. I told you that."

"I just wanted to make sure you were all right," Drake said.

"I have never needed your protection, especially as in general that protection was needed against you," Daisy persisted. "You have always been an evil-minded little man who tried to use me and to control me. So, you came here to destroy my business, did you? To destroy everything I had put together and my happiness?"

"It's not like that, Daisy. It's just you're better with me. You shouldn't be here. You need me."

"I have never needed you," Daisy said firmly. "The day I realised that was the day that I was free from you."

"Let's bring him inside and wait for the police to arrive and question him properly," O'Harris declared.

"I can't believe you turned out to be a murderer," Daisy sniffed. "Oh wait, actually I can. There was always something wicked about you. Something that given the right nudge could turn you into a madman."

"Please Daisy, I never hurt anybody."

Daisy was not interested in hearing any more of his lies. She turned around and stormed into the house. Edward followed her, leaving the others to frog march Drake into the property. They agreed they did not wish to spend any more time with him than was necessary, so once they were in the kitchen, they shut him in the pantry, which had a door that could be bolted. They then sat around the kitchen table on guard, waiting for the police to turn up.

Leaving the boys to guard Mr Drake in the pantry, Clara set off to see Mrs Geneva. She found her in the sitting room where Daisy and Annie had taken her. The woman did not look like a typical grieving widow. She sat dried eyed on the sofa and was helping herself to the tea and biscuits that Annie had kindly provided. If she was in shock, she was hiding it well.

"Hello again," Clara said to them as she came into the room, her words directed at Mrs Geneva.

Mrs Geneva glanced up from the biscuit she was then consuming. She smiled back at Clara and seemed wholly undisturbed by the fact that her husband had just been found deceased on the tennis courts.

In actual fact, she looked as if she was just enjoying a nice cup of tea with friends and that she had no woes in the world at all.

Clara was somewhat perturbed to see this. How could a woman who had suffered such a terrible loss such a short time ago act so calmly? It was either sheer denial and the woman was exhibiting some unusual form of shock, or she did not care that her husband was dead. Yet she had seemingly cared enough to come and speak to Daisy and ask her to look for her husband.

Annie moved up on the sofa to allow space for Clara to sit down. The look on her face suggested she was having similar thoughts to her friend. They exchanged glances and then Clara directed all her attention on Mrs Geneva.

"I am very sorry for your loss," she began, as it was the standard way to go about these things.

"It has been very unexpected," Mrs Geneva replied, munching away on a biscuit. "I do apologise for my manners. I always get hungry when something has upset me."

"Can I ask when you last saw your husband?" Clara continued knowing she only had a short amount of time before the police arrived and interrupted her questioning.

"I suppose it was about half seven," Mrs Geneva explained. "That was when he commented he had to go out for his evening walk. He can never sleep if he doesn't have his walk."

Mrs Geneva paused.

"I suppose that doesn't matter now."

She said this in all too cheery a manner, as if it amused her rather than distressed her. Clara was starting to think the woman might be a little peculiar.

"Did you see him once he was outside?" Clara asked her.

Mrs Geneva shook her head.

"He told me he was going towards the cliffs to get some sea air. As soon as he was gone, I went back to the book I was reading."

"What time was it when you realised he hadn't returned?" Clara said.

Mrs Geneva thought about this for a moment.

"I suppose it was about eight forty-five," she answered. "I had been quite absorbed in my book and was not really noting the time or how long he had been gone, but it was around then I looked up and realised he was not back. That seemed unusual. In general, he did not go for more than around forty-five minutes or so. He only has so much stamina."

Mrs Geneva was still talking about her husband as if he were alive. It didn't seem to have quite sunk into her as yet that he was gone.

"That was when you went down and saw Miss Belle," Clara continued.

"Actually, I think the first thing I did was go to the window and peer out. Our room overlooks the back garden, and I thought I would just see if I could spot him walking back. As it was, I couldn't see much at all because it was so dark. That's when I came downstairs and thought about speaking to Miss Belle. After what she had told us, I did feel slightly guilty that my husband had disobeyed her instructions."

"Where were you and Mr Geneva when the incident happened with Mr Hercules?" Clara asked her next.

It seemed logical that the two incidents were linked. The second one certainly seemed to cast doubt on the first being a random bear attack. Of course, it could be that the second attack was trying to imitate the first in an effort to throw them off the trail. She had a hunch there was a link between them, a connection she had not yet seen. Something that would explain the motive behind these killings.

"We were in the sea," Mrs Geneva said promptly. "Just splashing

about, really. We were with that other couple. They are known as Mr
and Mrs Hemisphere."

"You saw nothing out of the ordinary during that time?"

"No, nothing that was troubling. No sign of a bear if that's what
you mean. We didn't know about Mr Hercules until we were all back
at the house. Such a sad incident. He would go walking on the cliffs
alone often. How easy it would have been for him to just stumbled
over the edge. If you ask me, he was a troubled man. Someone
suggested that maybe he fell, and the bear came along later. I think that
is a very logical assumption. Brooding, that's the way I would describe
him. Always something on his mind."

"You knew Mr Hercules outside of the Sun Club?" Clara asked,
wondering if there might be a link that way between the pair.

Mrs Geneva shook her head.

"I didn't know anybody aside from my husband until we arrived
here. It's been very nice making new friends."

Mrs Geneva was not being much help and she still seemed to be
far too carefree for someone who had just lost a husband, in Clara's
opinion.

"Did anybody have any problems with Mr Geneva that you knew
about?" Clara said, knowing that now she was getting into dangerous
territory.

It was one thing to ask questions about where Mr Geneva had been
before he had died, and another to start delving into the matter of
motive.

Mrs Geneva looked at her curiously.

"I am not sure what you are implying. As far as I was aware, he'd
never had trouble with bears before."

Clara knew she was going to have to break her next piece of news
gently. Though she wasn't sure it would actually shock the woman to

learn her husband had been murdered any worse than she was already suffering.

"Mr Geneva was not killed by a bear," she explained carefully. "He was actually stabbed, and the claw marks were designed to disguise what had really happened."

"How extraordinary," Mrs Geneva said, once more displaying that she was quite unruffled by the matter at hand. "You mean to say that someone killed him and then a bear came along and scratched at him? How unfortunate for him."

That was not quite what Clara meant, but she decided not to drag over the matter.

"That brings me back to my point, Mrs Geneva," Clara persisted. "I was just wondering who might wish to see your husband dead?"

Clara was being blunt now, trying to nudge the woman into some sort of realisation of what was going on. She was finding Mrs Geneva's entire attitude rather disturbing.

"Oh, but I don't think anybody we know would want to kill him," Mrs Geneva said calmly. "My husband was quite a dear man. Quiet, inoffensive. No one said a bad word against him."

That was wholly unhelpful, it also seemed to be all they were going to get from Mrs Geneva. She had already gone back to stuffing biscuits in her mouth and drinking more tea.

"One last thing, if you wouldn't mind Mrs Geneva, might I have a quick look at your husband's belongings?"

This did cause Mrs Geneva to startle and to stop smiling.

"Why ever would you wish to do something like that?" She demanded.

"I was just considering whether it may be the case that there's something among your husband's belongings that could explain what happened here."

"I do not give you permission to look amongst my husband's personal items," Mrs Geneva said coldly, and her tone had turned hard so suddenly that she seemed a different person. "There is nothing among them that could possibly be relevant to this matter, so you can just keep your nose out of our room."

That told Clara rather firmly, and the sudden change of demeanour in the woman took them all by surprise. Clara, however, was not going to allow it to trouble her. She thanked Mrs Geneva for her time and rose. She nodded to Daisy and the pair of them headed out into the hallway while Annie remained with Mrs Geneva, trying to think what to say to the non-grieving widow.

Out in the hallway, Clara motioned for Daisy to head towards the staircase where they could talk in relative privacy.

"If I'm going to dive deeper into this matter and figure out what is going on, I need to look at Mr O'Brien's belongings," she said to her. "Are they still here?"

"Well, yes. No one has come to claim them. I'm not actually sure to whom I would send them."

"I shall need to go through them, see if there's something there that can explain why he was killed, and maybe explain why Mr Geneva was then murdered."

Daisy looked shocked at this turn of events, a slight tremble going through her body.

"You must do what you have to."

Clara smiled at her, trying to be reassuring.

"I also want to discuss with you, Mr Drake," she said. "I appreciate it's a sensitive topic, but just between me and you, I wanted to know what happened. He says you were engaged."

"We were, Clara. Possibly one of the worst decisions of my life," Daisy shook her head. "I was younger then and naive. Also, I was feeling somewhat adrift in this life. You see, I have money, but I don't have any family and that can make you reckless when it comes to your emotions. I was looking for someone to cling to, to be a rock for me, and I thought that might be Mr Drake. But Victor was never a rock. He was always trying to put me down. He feared that he would lose me, I think, and so he was always berating me, criticising me, making me feel small so that I would have to depend upon him. He was trying to destroy me, so that he could save me."

"That makes perfect sense considering what he has since said to us, and the type of man I can see him to be. You were wise to get away from him."

"It was far from easy," Daisy shook her head. "I was desperate to escape, and I began joining different hobby groups to try to make new friends. Victor was very negative about me having friends. Anything that I did on my own he was scathing about. But there was a part of me that desired to do things alone and salvage some of the independence I had had before I met him. I pushed myself on and worked in secret so that he wouldn't know what I was doing. I joined a local rambling society. I liked the idea of going for long walks and I thought he could hardly criticise what I was doing if he ever discovered it. As it happened, Edward had joined recently as well. As the two newest members, we sort of fell together. We didn't know the routes like everybody else did or the way things worked, and we were always helping each other out.

"Edward was so entirely different to Victor. He helped me. He praised me. He laughed at my jokes, and he never criticised me. We started out purely as friends, but through that friendship I realised how poisonous the relationship I had with Victor was. I realised I had to get away. You may not believe me, but I did not become romantically involved with Edward until my engagement was over, and even then it didn't happen at once. At the time, I was not thinking I was leaving Victor for Edward. Rather, I just was escaping him to begin my life anew."

"It is fortunate you came to that decision before you were married, otherwise you would have had a far more difficult time escaping him."

"You are quite right. Because we were only engaged, I was able to break things off and save my financial situation. I did not lose all the money I had inherited from my parents. It was a lucky escape. After that I decided I wanted to do something different, something radical that was just about me and that is how the Sun Club came into being. Edward was interested in the subject too. We had discussed it while we were on our walks. It was a little bit of a joke between us how both of us quite fancied the idea of wandering the countryside without our clothes on. It sounds rather crass when I say it out loud, but it was nothing like that. It was romantic. It was freedom. It was being one with the world."

"I am not going to judge you over that," Clara smiled at her. "I won't say it's my cup of tea. I prefer to be fully clad when I'm going out and about. But if that's the way you wish to live your lives and you're not causing harm to anyone, I do not see the problem."

Daisy nodded her head, relieved that Clara had understood her.

"The problem, as you can see, is not everyone is as agreeable as you are, Clara. Maybe someone is committing these murders to threaten our guests so that no one will come?"

"That is a possibility, though a rather extreme response. No one I have met so far has struck me as the sort to commit murder."

"That is good of you to say so, Clara, but what else could there possibly be? If this is not about someone trying to destroy what I am doing, then, what is the motive?"

"That is why I want to look through Mr Hercules' belongings.

Maybe there is something there that can give me a hint as to what is going on. Perhaps someone wanted Mr Hercules and Mr Geneva dead for other reasons. For that matter, I need to look into their backgrounds outside of the Sun Club and I would appreciate it if you would give me Mr Geneva's real name."

"I don't know if I can," Daisy shook her head. "Mrs Geneva, after all, is still alive and it wouldn't just be about revealing her husband's true entity, but about revealing hers. We pride ourselves on anonymity here at the Sun Club."

"Yet if we don't solve this mystery, there won't be a Sun Club for there to be anonymity. And if someone is using that anonymity as a means to cover up a crime then who are you really helping, Daisy?"

Daisy shook her head again, troubled by it all but realising that Clara had a fair point.

"I shall think about it," she said.

It was a start.

Chapter Twenty-Nine

"I f you can show me to Mr O'Brien's room, I shall make a start up there," Clara said.

Daisy agreed to this and escorted Clara up the staircase, showing her along the hallway to room number five which was where Mr O'Brien had spent his brief time at the Sun Club.

Clara entered the room and noted how well appointed it was, the tall bay windows allowed in a good deal of light during the day, and it was spacious with an area set aside as a sitting room, the bed in the middle and then, to the far side, another area where there was a desk and dressing table. To the side of that was a door that led into a private bathroom. The Sun Club certainly treated its guests well.

"Should I stay?" Daisy asked, hovering at the doorway. "Or is it more proper that I go back? I don't know what to do."

"You can leave me to it," Clara said. "There is nothing you need to protect here, not with Mr O'Brien being deceased. Go back and wait for the police."

Daisy nodded and departed, leaving Clara in peace to carry on with her investigating. That was exactly how Clara liked it. She could now think for herself and take her time without someone looking over her shoulder and interrupting her. The first thing she did was wander around the room and get a feel for it. You could tell a lot from a room on a first glance, even when it was a place someone had only briefly stayed in. The character of a person came with them, and it very quickly imprinted onto a room. It did not take long to pick up a few ideas about Mr O'Brien.

The way he had discarded clothing across the floor showed that he was either someone who was used to having people picking up behind him or didn't much care about where he left things. A large shaving kit was laid out on the dressing table, indicating that he was someone who prided himself on his appearance. The bed had been made-up by Daisy, so she could not take any clues from that, but she did note how the cushions on the sofa were still in slight disarray from the last time Mr O'Brien had been here. Two cushions had been placed on the left side of the sofa, suggesting he had been laying back on it. Clara walked over and saw that there was a book lying open on the floor, tucked just beneath the chair, she reached down and pulled it out. It was a book on philosophy and the way its many pages were dog eared suggested it was one that Mr O'Brien had read frequently. She took a glance at the page he had left it on, wondering if it might offer a hint of something about the man. But the discussions in the paragraphs before her were somewhat tiresome and tedious, so she gave up on it quite quickly and placed the book on the sofa. What she needed to look for were personal items, ones that could give her clues as to Mr O'Brien's day-to-day life; who he knew, who he associated with, and anybody who might have a dark past.

She headed over to the desk and examined its contents to see if there were any letters or a diary that could hint at what Mr O'Brien was up to. She found that it was virtually untouched, though Daisy supplied all her guests with a large amount of stationary and pens in case they wished to write letters while they were at the Sun Club. Presumably, Mr O'Brien had not been there long enough to warrant writing a note to someone. She next went to the drawers in the bedside tables and checked to see if there was anything in them. The first thing she noted in the one on the left-hand side was an envelope. She took it out and saw that it was addressed to Mr O'Brien and not his pseudonym. She pulled out the letter from within and saw that it was from a friend inviting him to this very Sun Club, suggesting that he come along and even supplying a name of someone he could bring with him as his companion. This was curious seeing as the Sun Club regulation meant that people brought their spouses along with them. The way things were stated in the letter, it almost seemed as though the writer was implying that O'Brien invite someone to go with him to masquerade as his spouse.

Why would he go to such trouble? Clara scanned through the letter for anything else but didn't noticed anything of interest. She finally glanced at the name at the bottom. It had been written to Mr O'Brien by Mr James Gordon. Unfortunately, she did not know which of the guests that name might relate to or if it related to a guest at all, though the implication on the letter suggested that whoever had written this intended for O'Brien to be there at the same time as themselves.

She stared at the name for a moment and wondered whether Mr Geneva had picked his name based on the fact that both Geneva and Gordon bore the same first letter. If that was the case, was this a connection between the two men? It would certainly mean that Mrs Geneva was lying. She hoped she could persuade Daisy to reveal their true identity to her. At least that would rule them out in this regard if nothing else. She put the letter back in the drawer. She could not take anything away as the police might search this place too and she didn't want to remove evidence that they would need to see.

She headed around the bed and started to explore the other bedside table, which offered her nothing in regard to more clues about Mr O'Brien. It contained a handful of pill bottles of the usual sort that people took when they were travelling; digestion tablets and headache pills. There was nothing particularly insightful there.

She finally located Mr O'Brien's suitcase under the bed and pulled it out. It was not locked, and it sprang open easily enough. There were more clothes carefully folded up inside. She went through them, taking them out and putting them to one side so that she could examine the suitcase properly. Beneath them, she found a hairbrush that had yet to be put out on the dressing table, some clean socks and a couple more books also on philosophy. One she was curious to see was a translation from Ancient Greek. The title she did not know and when she dived into the book a bit deeper, she was surprised to see that there were an awful lot of essays on the act of sodomy. She thought about this for a moment. The Greeks, of course, were known to have been rather casual about their sexual relations and were not particularly adverse about who they went with. However, it was not the sort of book you expected to see in an English gentleman's holiday luggage. It was the sort that might be studied at a university for academic reasons or secretly in a private library. Why was it here? It raised an interesting question in Clara's mind.

She had a book that was philosophising about sodomy, and she knew full well that there were men around who were inclined to that behaviour. She also had a letter from Mr James Gordon inviting Mr O'Brien here and suggesting he supplied himself with a fake wife to get past the regulations of the Sun Club. Certain patterns were starting to come together. Could it be that O'Brien had come here for an assignation with another man? Or was she reading too much into an innocent letter and a copy of an old book? She placed them back in the suitcase along with the clothes, and then searched the pockets that were in the top lining of the lid. She didn't find much at first, until she pulled out another small envelope. When she examined the item closer, she realised it contained photography negatives. She held them up to the dim light from the fittings on the ceiling and tried to see what was going on in the picture. She thought she could make out some gentlemen in the scene.

The envelope had no writing on it and did not indicate who the picture was of, or why it had been brought there.

She decided the best thing to do would be to show them to Oliver and see if he could make copies from the negative. It may give them a hint of what was going on. Yet that would mean removing the items from the suitcase, and she'd already said to herself she wasn't going to remove any potential evidence the police would want to see. She struggled with this moral dilemma. Clara liked to be as cooperative with the police as she could be. Inspector Park-Coombs had always been very supportive of her, and she didn't want to break his trust. But she desperately wanted to find out what was in these pictures. A notion then came to her.

Captain O'Harris had his car here and Oliver was, after all, the police photographer. If they were going to ask anybody to make up copies of these pictures, it would be him. So, wasn't she just helping them out in that regard? She would ask O'Harris to run Oliver back into Brighton and collect all his photography gear. They would set up a temporary darkroom somewhere in the house, and he could process these negatives, right here. Copies could be given to the police when they arrived, and Clara would have some too. It would mean the evidence didn't have to actually leave the Sun Club.

It was a good compromise.

Clara put everything back and headed downstairs to speak to Oliver and arrange the matter.

Chapter Thirty

The men were still all in the kitchen, talking among themselves and smoking. Mr Drake could be heard making small protests from the pantry, complaining that it was damp and dark, and that he was sure a mouse had just run over his foot. Occasionally he asked if he might have a cup of tea. They were ignoring him.

"I have a request for you, John, and also Oliver," Clara said as she entered the room.

Both men looked up at her.

"What are you thinking?" O'Harris asked.

"I found some photography negatives up in Mr O'Brien's room. I'd like to see what they show when they are developed, but I can't really take the negatives away from here. I wondered if you'd be good enough, John, to take Oliver back to Brighton so he could get his developing gear. The police would probably want copies as well."

"Not a bad idea, actually," Oliver said. "The police will want me to take pictures of the crime scene and I don't have my camera here. I was going to wait until they arrived and see if I could get a lift back into Brighton. But it would be useful if I could get ahead of things. It would save them a lot of time."

O'Harris nodded at this logic. He rose and went off with Oliver to head back into the town. Clara was left alone with Tommy and Peterson. Edward had once again departed. It was not clear where he had gone but he had stated that he could not remain anywhere near Mr Drake. The man's mere voice and incessant whining had started to cause him to lose his temper.

"Did you find anything in Mr O'Brien's room that could suggest why he was killed?" Tommy asked his sister, dropping his voice to a whisper so that Drake could not overhear.

"Nothing conclusive. Just a few scraps of information that might be significant. It seems that someone suggested he come here with a fake wife to bypass the rules of the Sun Club. If he did that, I have to ask why?"

"Maybe he was just a very keen naturist who happened to be single," Tommy suggested.

"I suppose that's a possibility, but some other items I found in his room suggested that it could be that Mr O'Brien came here for an assignation."

"Now that would go completely against the Sun Club rules," Tommy said, raising an eyebrow and thinking of what Daisy would make of such a thing. "It would make it seem as though the Sun Club was here for people to cavort about and explore their innermost desires."

"And it would make it even worse to certain minds that, from what I saw in Mr O'Brien's personal belongings, the assignation here may not have been with a woman."

Peterson had been sitting quietly, allowing them to talk without interfering. Now he raised his head, curious.

Tommy, however, was the one who spoke.

"Are you saying that Mr O'Brien was here to meet with a man?"

"That seems to be a possibility," Clara agreed. "And I can't help but wonder if that man was Mr Geneva. Could this all be connected?"

"Come off it," Tommy said, almost chuckling. "You did see O'Brien? I mean, he was a well-built young man. Now compare him to Mr Geneva. He was an older man, well past his best, somewhat flabby around the edges, certainly not handsome."

"Since when did romance require people to be beautiful?" Clara reminded him. "If that was the way of the world, there would be an awful lot of people who would never find love."

"My point is the disparity between them. They didn't look like two who could be a pair."

"Well, maybe that is true. All I'm saying is that the conclusion that seems to be suggesting itself to me by what I have found in his luggage is that O'Brien was here to meet a man. There is also the curious behaviour of Mrs Geneva; she is not acting as you would expect a grieving widow."

Peterson at last spoke up.

"I noticed that myself," he said. "When I was consoling her, she didn't seem particularly upset. You would expect someone whose husband is lying dead on the tennis courts to be at least tearful, even if they were able to contain themselves. She didn't show a hint of emotion. She leaned on me for sure. But it seemed more because she was tired rather than because she was upset."

"It all makes for some very interesting possibilities," Clara nodded. "I'm not as yet sure where they lead us."

From the pantry they heard a strange, high-pitched voice. Mr Drake was finally losing his patience and was prepared to wheedle to get his way out of the pantry.

"I have thought of some information that might be useful to you," he called. "If you would just let me out so I could have a cup of tea."

They did not immediately release Drake because they were not convinced he did have anything useful to say. He was the sort who would lie to get his way.

"If you are suggesting you have suddenly come up with some notion about what is going on here, I'm afraid I don't believe you," Tommy said to him sternly. "You've been whining and complaining the whole time you've been in there, saying all manner of stuff just to try and get us to take you out."

"That doesn't mean I don't know anything useful," Mr Drake called out through the door.

"You forget you are yourself suspected of being behind these murders," Tommy pointed out. "We're not ignoring that possibility."

"But I didn't. Honestly, I didn't. However, I think I might have seen something. Please let me speak up."

"Tell us what you think you know and if we believe you we will let you out for a cup of tea," Clara bargained.

Behind the pantry door, they could hear some shuffling, and something muttered under the breath as if Mr Drake were swearing to himself.

"I won't tell you anything unless you let me out immediately. It's stuffy in here. I'm having trouble breathing."

"There is a gap under the door," Tommy remarked. "Wide enough to allow plenty of air through."

"Well, I don't like it. Its dark. You should let me out. I can tell you all sorts of things."

"The problem is, we don't believe you," Clara said to him. "You have been lying to us all evening. Why should we suddenly think you are telling the truth?"

"Because I am. Because I will. Please just give me a chance."

"You have to offer something better than that," Tommy huffed.

"All right, how about this. You let me out and I will tell you my information. If you decide that it isn't worth your time, you can put me straight back in here. Just let me have a chance to take a breath of fresh air and get some light, and maybe a cup of tea."

"He has been harping on about a cup of tea for the last hour," Peterson said, grumbling.

"How do we know you won't try and make a bolt for it before the police get here?" Clara remarked, still not moving from the table.

"My hands are still tied," Drake replied. "It would be very difficult for to get away like that."

"He has a point in that regard," Tommy nodded.

"Very well. We will let you out to come sit at the table and tell us what you think you know. But if you try to escape, or you lie to us once more, you are going straight back into the pantry," Clara told him. "I make no promises that if you annoy me, you won't go back in there anyway."

"I will be as good as gold," Drake promised.

Peterson snorted at this information, clearly as disbelieving of it as they were. Tommy rose, and headed to the pantry, pulling back the bolt and then opening the door carefully. Drake was still sitting on the floor. He made no attempt to rush at Tommy or do anything that could have caused him harm. That, at least, was a good sign.

"Come on, then," Tommy said, grabbing him up by the arm and pulling him to his feet, before taking him to the kitchen table. He sat him down in a chair on the left side of Clara.

"What do you want to tell us?" Clara said.

Drake had such a look of gratitude on his face for her mercy it was hard to stomach. It was so insipid and irritating. He'd only been locked in a pantry after all, he acted as if she had rescued him from drowning.

"I really appreciate this," he said.

"You said you had information for us," Clara reminded him.

"I did say that," Mr Drake nodded. "And I meant it. I'm not a liar."

"Yes, you are," Tommy growled, his chin resting in his hand as he leaned his elbow on the table. He looked exhausted. Clara was sympathetic to that feeling. She was exhausted, too.

"If you're going to tell us anything, will you not just get on with it?" She said to Drake.

"Yes, you better hurry up or else we will begin to think that you told us you had information just to get out of the pantry."

"I really do have information," Drake insisted. "You promise you won't put me back in the pantry if I tell you?"

"I make no such promises," Clara informed him. "However, I will say this, if you give us the information and it is relevant to this case, we will make sure you have a cup of tea. And if you behave yourself, we won't shut you in the pantry immediately."

Drake realised this was the best he was going to get. He nodded his head and then braced himself.

"I saw someone outside. When I was..."

He didn't know quite how to finish that sentence, so Tommy finished it for him.

"While you were lurking in the bushes," he emphasised the word lurking.

Drake did not deny what he had been up to. Perhaps at last he was realising how bad things looked for him, and maybe he was even having a pang of conscience about everything. Though Clara was not hopeful on that front.

"I saw a person when I was around in the bushes," Drake continued.

"Was it a man?" Tommy asked him. "Was it Mr Geneva? Or was it O'Harris or Oliver?"

"No, you see, that is my point. It wasn't any of your people, and it wasn't Mr Geneva who, I have to say, I never saw coming out of the house or on the tennis courts for that matter. I never saw a bear wandering around either. If I had, I certainly would have run for it."

"That is probably the first honest thing you have said all evening," Clara replied cynically. "I do believe, Mr Drake, that had you seen a bear, you would have run faster than you had ever done in your life."

Drake did not seem to understand that she was implying he was a coward or else he didn't care.

"The person I saw was an older woman. She wasn't Daisy. I know her all too well. She was a larger woman wearing a dark overcoat and a hat. But I could see beneath the coat a flash of her dress and it looked to have a floral pattern."

Clara turned her attention to her brother. Drake had not seen Mrs Geneva at all that evening. She had claimed she had been upstairs while her husband was out walking the grounds.

"Where did you see this woman?" Clara asked him.

Though she was being careful not to indicate how excited she was by this news, Mr Drake immediately picked up on the fact that she was interested.

"I saw her on the main lawn," he said. "I had to duck behind some bushes, or I thought she might see me. I noticed that she was heading in the rough direction of the tennis courts."

"Do you know what time this was?" Tommy asked.

Drake was now put on the spot. He had not been keeping close track of the time. He thought about things for a moment.

"It was not long after I had returned from speaking to you," he said. "I decided I would ride immediately here. You had upset me and made me angry. I came at once and I hid my bicycle by the side wall and then I climbed over into the woods and headed across to the house. By the time that all happened, it must have been getting on for about quarter past eight. I had not been long hanging around before I saw the woman. I suppose that would make it about eight twenty."

"Tell us what she was doing," Clara spoke. "Did you see her return to the house?"

"I did," Drake replied. "She wasn't gone very long at all. She disappeared into the darkness. I wasn't paying attention to her after that. I was more interested in the house, trying to get close to the window, to the room where I could see a light on. I knew Daisy must be in there. I can say it was no more than five minutes before the woman returned, which was irritating because I had just moved out of my hiding space. She hastened back into the house. There was one thing I noticed. She no longer had her overcoat on. She appeared to have discarded it completely and in the flimsy moonlight I could see her dress even clearer. As she reached the back door, the light in the kitchen gave me a quick glimpse of the bright floral patterns on her dress and her rounded face."

"I wonder what she did with the overcoat," Tommy said to his sister.

"She lied to us completely," Clara shook her head. "Now I think about it, she was so calm when she spoke of her husband and his death. She seemed almost, dare I say it, pleased."

"Are you thinking what I am thinking?" Tommy asked. "That Mrs Geneva somehow had a role in her husband's death."

"Well, I would like to find that overcoat. We said to ourselves that the killer must have been splattered with blood. If she was wearing that overcoat, it would have protected her dress, which we saw her in later and clearly was unstained. But the coat itself would be marked. She would have hidden it somewhere."

"But where?"

They both cast their attention towards Private Peterson. He had been quiet throughout the discussion with Drake, but they knew he had been paying sharp attention. When they looked in his direction, Peterson gave them a smile.

"I have spent a great deal of time mapping out these grounds in my head. I always do something like that. We were taught to do that at the Front. When you get to a new area you need to check where any enemy positions might be. Know the landscape as best as you can. Anyway, I can give you a good idea about some suitable hiding places around the tennis courts."

"We need to look for that overcoat at once," Tommy nodded. "Sorry, Mr Drake, but you're going back into the pantry while we're busy."

"Wait, but you promised me a cup of tea," Drake said, looking at them appalled. "And I was very helpful to you."

If he expected sympathy from them, he was to be disappointed. Clara had no time left for the man.

"We shall make you a cup of tea and you can have it in the pantry," she said. "In the meantime, we have work to do and a killer to stop. We can't allow Mrs Geneva out of our sight."

"You think she might bolt?" Tommy suggested.

"I think when she realises that we are investigating her, she may very well attempt to get away. We'll put Mr Drake in the pantry and then we'll have Annie, Mrs Geneva and Daisy sit here in the kitchen under the guise of keeping an eye on him, while the rest of us go outside to search for the missing raincoat."

Drake had been looking deflated before, but now he heard that his Daisy would be in the kitchen with him he brightened up immediately.

"We should put Edward in here as well," Clara said firmly. "Just to make sure Mr Drake doesn't try to wheedle his way around Daisy. On the other hand, he will have to face the wrath of Annie if he does. You haven't met her yet, have you, Mr Drake? Do not be surprised if she takes very badly towards you."

Drake did not appreciate how fearsome Annie could be when she was moved, and so he did not appreciate the threat. He would soon enough find out.

They did at least make him a cup of tea before putting him and his teacup back into the pantry and making sure the door was bolted. Then they went to talk to the others.

Chapter
Thirty-One

C lara did not want to alert Mrs Geneva to what they were up to,
so she came up with a story to explain why she wanted the three
women to remove themselves to the kitchen.

"I thought I heard a noise outside. It might be someone else lurking
around. Just in case, we think we ought to take a look outside. Could
you ladies perhaps go into the kitchen and just keep an eye on Mr
Drake? I will ask Edward to assist as well."

Daisy did not look impressed at the thought of being in the
company of her ex-fiancé. Clara would have liked to tell her the truth
as to why she needed her to go into the kitchen, but at that moment in
time, she couldn't. Mrs Geneva was right there, and she was looking
at Clara with that vague smile on her face.

"We hopefully won't be long. O'Harris and Oliver will be back
soon, and the police will be here anytime now. You could hand Drake
over to them immediately."

Daisy nodded at this, though she still seemed unconvinced.

Tommy had headed upstairs and found Edward once again in his study. He brought him back downstairs to join with the others and they sent them into the kitchen.

"Annie," Clara called her over just before they were about to head out into the gardens, "I know you will keep a firm eye on Drake and make sure he gets up to no mischief. If he causes any bother to anyone, you have my full permission to do your worst."

Annie smiled broadly at her.

"I shall do my very worst if he causes me trouble," she promised before heading into the kitchen and reaching out for Daisy's arm to reassure her.

Clara was not entirely surprised to see that a friendship was forming between them. Annie might say some things and argue about her principles, but when it came down to it, she took people at face value. She had clearly decided that Daisy was worthy of her affections.

Leaving them all behind, and with Mrs Geneva now happily settled at the kitchen table and consuming yet more tea and biscuits, Clara, Tommy, and Private Peterson headed outside into the gardens. They let Peterson lead the way. He was like a dog on a trail, leading them directly to what he thought would be a good hiding spot for a coat. They had to walk past the body of Mr Geneva, but that did not bother them entirely. It was not their first corpse, after all and if you didn't look too closely, you could pretend the man had just fallen asleep.

The first spot that Peterson brought them to was another area of bushes. He indicated that behind them there was a small dip in the ground.

"Earlier I took a closer look around here, thinking it could be a hiding spot for someone. I realised it was a disused drainage system and the flowers must have been grown around it to try and cover it." There was a cover over the drain, but it appeared to be only loosely covering the hole. Peterson reached through the bushes as he spoke and easily wrenched up the old lid of the drain. They looked down into the dingy hole but couldn't see anything.

Tommy flashed his torch into the deep space, and they examined the spot as closely as they could. There was no sign of a coat.

"Mrs Geneva probably didn't even know about this drain," Clara gently explained to Peterson, not wishing to diminish his efforts. "We need something a little bit more obvious."

Peterson nodded his head in understanding, then he directed them to another place, just to the back of the tennis courts. There they found an old wooden chest for storing tennis rackets and balls. It was not locked and all of the guests at the house would have known about it. They opened it to see if anything was inside but all they revealed were more rackets and the other items for playing sports outside.

"Next place," Tommy said to Peterson.

Peterson led them a little further away, and this time they came to an old statue in the garden. It was that of a young woman holding a large ewer from which had once poured water. More recently it had been used as a flowerpot, though right at that moment the vase was empty. Peterson pointed out how hollow and deep the stone ewer was. How someone could easily hide something in it.

Tommy flashed his torch up onto the vase. They couldn't see anything at first, then Clara thought she spied something deep in the shadows of the pot.

The ewer was over their heads, and Peterson was the tallest, so he plunged his hand inside and felt around. After a torturously long moment, when no expression crossed Peterson's face other than deep concentration, he sharply pulled something out.

The item was bundled up and wedged deep in the stone vase. He had to yank hard to remove it. What fell out was a long raincoat.

It had been shoved hastily into the vase. Considering the short stature of Mrs Geneva, it would not have been easy to get it in there, but it had been a good hiding place. No one would have really considered looking in there, at least not at night when the shadows masked the fact that the vase was hollow. Mrs Geneva would have had time the next day, before the police conducted a more thorough search, to move the raincoat further away.

They unfolded the coat on the ground. Tommy shone his torch across it and there across the breast of the coat they saw great splashes of blood.

Clara stared and stared at the sight. Somehow, she wasn't surprised at what had happened. She had seen on Mrs Geneva's face something that was almost akin to madness. Even so, it was hard to imagine the plump, pleasant-faced woman sitting in the kitchen had taken up a knife and stabbed her husband.

"If Mrs Geneva is still here, then the knife ought to be still here too," Clara said. "She has either discarded it somewhere around the bushes, or she has hidden it in the house."

Peterson was fumbling in the vase further when he pulled out his hand. This time he had a handkerchief in it. It was covered in blood.

"I would surmise that she wiped the blade clean with this, and then she took it with her."

"We need to search her room," Clara said. "If there's a knife among the bushes we can leave that to the police constables to find when it is light again tomorrow. We already have proof enough of what she did."

"We have proof," Tommy said. "But we have no motive. Why did she kill her husband? Do we presume she also killed Mr O'Brien?"

"That brings me back to my previous supposition," Clara said. "Not that I can prove that Mr Geneva and Mr O'Brien were in a relationship, and they conspired to come here to pursue that relationship."

"That would be motive for Mrs Geneva to lash out at them. She would not only feel betrayed, but she would be fearful for her own reputation."

"Hell, hath no fury like a woman scorned," Peterson nodded. "How many times have we heard of stories of women attacking their husbands because they had a mistress?"

"A mistress Mrs Geneva could probably have lived with. Worst case scenario, she could have got a divorce from her husband. But how can you get a divorce when the reason for it is because your husband is seeing another man? Imagine the scandal," Clara remarked.

"More to the point, they had embroiled her in their affair," Tommy said. "She had been dragged along to this place as a cover for what they were up to. Remember the rules, Mr Geneva had to bring a spouse here. Mr O'Brien bent the rules and got away with it because of his influence. But Mr Geneva could not have banked on that being the same for him, not to mention it would have looked strange that two different men failed to bring their spouses. So, he brought his wife as an excuse to pretend that everything was above board. She must have felt so used."

"They certainly did not treat her fairly or justly," Clara agreed. "That doesn't absolve her from the fact that she has committed two brutal murders. If we assume she killed Mr O'Brien as well."

"And that is a lot of assumptions with very little proof. All we can say for certain is that Mrs Geneva left the house in this raincoat and then hid it when it became covered in blood. She could always claim that she saw her husband lying on the tennis court and went to his aid and that was how the blood came to be on her coat."

"I don't think such an excuse would stand up in court, but I get your point. I think we need to confront her with this. Then we need to find out exactly what is going on in this house."

"Whatever is going on, it's not going to look good for Daisy and Edward," Tommy shook his head.

"We shall have to cross that bridge when we come to it. It may be possible to avoid anything coming out in the papers. We shall have to see. In any case, we cannot avoid the truth just because it might be unseemly."

They were all agreed on that as they headed back to the house.

The others were still in the kitchen when they arrived. Mrs Geneva had now sated herself on biscuits and was sitting quietly dozing in a wooden chair by the large range. Daisy stood up the second Clara came in.

"Did you see any signs of someone out there?"

"We didn't see anybody," Clara explained, "but we did find some new evidence."

She was watching Mrs Geneva the entire time she spoke; the woman did not open her eyes. She had her hands resting across her rotund belly and seemed quite settled in her sleep.

"Daisy, Edward, we know who killed Mr Geneva," Clara spoke softly. "We just don't have the evidence to prove it."

Peterson held up the raincoat. Its blood-stained front clearly visible. Though the blood had now gone a dingy brown colour as it had dried, there was no mistaking what it was. Daisy gasped. Edward's jaw dropped sharply.

"That's a man's raincoat. So, he did do it. Drake is responsible for this."

There was a whimper from the pantry.

"It wasn't me. I didn't do it!"

"I don't believe Mr Drake did this," Clara said firmly. "Though, of course, he could have been lying about what he saw. I suppose that comes down to you, Mrs Geneva."

Clara was still watching the woman by the range. Mrs Geneva had opened her eyes and the quiet smile on her face had faded. Now she had a stern, mean expression on her face.

"Daisy, I would like permission to search your guest's room. I think we may find a knife in there."

Mrs Geneva rose to her feet sharply.

"That would be an invasion of my privacy. You'll never hear the end of this Miss Belle if you allow such a thing."

Daisy was flummoxed, not sure what to do.

"Are you suggesting that this raincoat belongs to Mrs Geneva?"

"I have never seen that coat in my life," Mrs Geneva said firmly.

"I don't suppose it actually belongs to you, Mrs Geneva. Or should I say, Mrs Gordon?"

Clara waited to see what response this information would get. Mrs Geneva did not reveal anything, but Daisy gave a start.

"Did you go behind my back, Clara, and look in my guest register to see their real names?"

"No, I didn't, Daisy. But you have just confirmed that my surmise was correct. I found evidence in Mr O'Brien's room that he knew a gentleman named James Gordon. I surmised that might have been Mrs Gordon's husband. O'Brien and Gordon had a very close relationship."

Mrs Geneva huffed loudly but said no more.

"I'm going to also surmise that this coat belongs to Mr Gordon. Now we have it inside, it may be possible to find a label on it that identifies it as his property," Clara motioned to Peterson, who put the coat on the table.

He started to turn it out, looking for any labels within it. It did not take long to find a laundry label that had the initials J.G. on it.

"James Gordon," Clara nodded. "Your husband, Mrs Gordon and

the lover of Mr O'Brien."

There was a gasp from around the room, but Mrs Geneva simply laughed at them.

"What nonsense you are spouting," she said. "You are suggesting my husband would do something so criminal, something so wicked, as to consort lasciviously with another man."

"We have proof of that in a letter that Mr O'Brien brought here," Clara told her.

"What are you saying, Clara?" Daisy said, her voice filled with despair.

"Mr Gordon and Mr O'Brien came here to have an illicit assignation. It was done to protect their identities, since no one else would know who they were, and because they both had an interest in the naturist movement. Not to mention they could hide some of the scandal by bringing spouses with them. For whatever reason, Mr O'Brien's pretend spouse decided not to attend. That could have left things in a pickle, except you were most accommodating about the matter, Daisy."

"Are you saying that I enabled them to do this?" Daisy asked in horror.

"Not wittingly, of course," Clara replied. "In any case, they were going to try and commit their subterfuge within your rules. I'm sorry, Daisy, but you've been used just as badly as Mrs Gordon has. But at least you didn't take a knife to the perpetrators."

"You know, it just occurred to me that there are a lot of knives in this kitchen," Tommy said. "I wonder if we were to take them all out and look at them, whether any of them might have traces of blood upon them?"

They all found themselves looking around the room. Annie rose from her seat.

"Leave me in charge of that," she said. "You go upstairs and search Mrs Gordon's room for any further evidence."

"This is preposterous," Mrs Gordon said loudly. "I demand that you do something about this, Miss Belle."

Daisy spun on her feet towards the woman. She was thinking to herself how Mrs Gordon had been so calm when she had learned her husband was dead.

"Did you do it, Mrs Gordon? Did you stab your husband?"

Mrs Gordon shook her head.

"You can't possibly be taking any of this nonsense seriously," she countered.

"I know what it is to be so angry with someone that anything seems possible," Daisy continued. "That the thought of taking up a knife and stabbing them through the heart suddenly has a great appeal to it."

From the direction of the pantry, there was another whimpering sound as Mr Drake realised who she was referring to.

Mrs Gordon was staring at them. She was trying to think of a way she could deny what was before her. Finally, she came to the one thing which was causing them still a problem.

"You have no real proof that my husband was involved with Mr O'Brien," she said firmly. "You mentioned a letter, but I don't suppose it's very explicit. For all I know, you're just making things up. In fact, I don't think you can prove anything."

She had a point. The letter was not really strong enough to stand up in a court of law on its own. She was about to say something more, but at that moment the door swung open.

O'Harris and Oliver had returned and hot on their heels were the police. As Inspector Park-Coombs strode into the house and called out to ask where everyone was, Clara knew it was time to hand things over to him. She waved him down the corridor and quickly apprised him of what was going on.

The inspector walked into the kitchen and stared at the assembled crowd. Mrs Gordon glowered at him.

"I demand that you make these people release me so I can go on my way and head home," she told the inspector. "I have had a very trying day. My husband is dead."

"Clara has explained things to me, and no one is leaving until I've seen everything and spoken to everyone," he nodded to Oliver. "I want those negatives you told me about. Print them up and see if they mean anything. In the meantime, I think everybody needs to explain to me what exactly is going on. Starting with you, Mrs Gordon."

Chapter
Thirty-Two

With the police taking over matters, Drake secured in the pantry and Mrs Gordon going nowhere, it seemed an appropriate time for some of them, at least, to get some rest. It had been a long day, and they were all pretty exhausted. Clara, Tommy, and Annie made their way back to the sitting room, where they curled themselves up on various pieces of furniture and had a quick nap. O'Harris was too alert to yet succumb to slumber, so he was assisting Oliver with developing the negatives they had come across. Daisy and Edward had retreated upstairs until they were needed for further questioning by the police.

It was getting towards dawn when Oliver finally appeared in the doorway of the sitting room. Clara, who was only lightly dozing, came immediately to attention and saw him there. O'Harris was just behind him.

"I've taken a copy of the pictures I developed to the police. I thought you might like to see one too," Oliver said.

He walked towards Clara handing over a freshly developed

photograph. She took it from him and saw a picture of three men. One she immediately recognised as Mr O'Brien. The other man, though younger in this image, was immediately recognisable as Mr Gordon. The years had obviously not been terribly kind to him, but his distinctive features had perhaps once offered him a rugged attraction.

"I believe this is the last piece of proof you need to confirm Mr Gordon and Mr O'Brien knew each other before they came here," Oliver said.

"Has she confessed?" Tommy asked aloud.

It was O'Harris who answered with a shake of his head.

"So far, she has said nothing. Inspector Park-Coombs says it is very frustrating. The circumstantial evidence is certainly enough to arrest her without her making a confession, though it might not be enough to convict her."

"I'm just sorry for Daisy and Edward. This is quite the scandal for them to endure," Clara sighed, sitting up and rubbing at her eyes. "It was bad enough a murder happening here. But now we know that the murder was a result of a homosexual relationship, which for some people will be even worse than the fact that someone was killed."

"It will certainly add grist to the mill for the Reverend Lane and his group," Tommy nodded. "But what can we do?"

"The police will probably attempt to keep as much of this out of the papers as possible," O'Harris answered him. "The Gordons are well respected, and their family has a long reach. It is in the best interests of everyone for things to be kept relatively quiet. Of course, the circumstances will have to come out in court."

"We will just have to do the best we can," Clara shrugged.

She then noticed that the spot that Annie had been curled up in just a short while ago was empty.

"Where did Annie go?"

"Annie's in the kitchen, whipping up breakfast for everyone," Oliver remarked. "She seemed to think we could all do with it."

Clara and Tommy joined them to wander back down to the kitchen. Mr Drake had been removed from the pantry. He was now wearing a pair of handcuffs and had a police constable keeping a close watch over him as he sat at the kitchen table. He was making appreciative noises as Annie prepared a breakfast consisting of bacon, eggs, fried bread, and sausages.

Mrs Gordon was also sitting at the table with the inspector. She had refused to answer most of his questions and was still in denial about everything. However, the evidence that his constables were turning up was proving most interesting. Tommy's guess that one of the kitchen knives had been used as the murder weapon was correct, and Annie had assisted in finding that particular knife before she had gone to take her rest. With the murder weapon now to hand, there was hope that they might find fingerprints on the handle that would identify Mrs Gordon as the killer. They had the evidence of Mr Drake to prove she had lied about where she was and that she must have seen her husband on the tennis court. And they had her husband's raincoat, which was covered in blood, and she had last been seen wearing it. Not to mention the picture which finally pulled together the motive for the crime. It was looking bad for Mrs Gordon.

Clara left him to it. Feeling she could do with a breath of fresh air. The day was cool and crisp outside, moisture hanging in the air and dripping off the leaves of the trees. There were several constables in the grounds, all swarming around the body on the tennis court. They were searching through the bushes and keeping a close watch on the body until Oliver could finish taking his photographs. Now that the light had returned, he would be taking as many as he could and then

Dr Deáth would arrive, and the body would be removed.

Clara was standing to one side of a veranda that ran around the back of the house watching them when she heard a strange noise in the bushes. It was halfway between a snuffle and the cry of a child. Tommy was just a couple of steps behind her. She motioned to him.

"Did you hear that?"

Tommy came and joined her, and they stood staring down into the bushes where she had heard the sound. Everything was quiet for a while and then there was another noise, same as before. Clara nudged her brother.

"What animal makes that sort of noise?"

"I don't know," Tommy replied.

There was now a faint whimpering sound coming from the bushes, as if whatever was in there was not terribly happy. Clara headed down the steps of the veranda and towards the shrubbery. She bent down before she got too close and tried to peer inside.

"Could it be a cat?" She said. "Cats can make all sorts of strange noises."

She started to purse together her lips and make cooing noises to lure out the cat. Something rustled in the leaves. It seemed to be working. The noises were attracting it.

"Maybe it's hungry," Tommy said. "Could be a feral cat."

"It could be injured," Clara added. "That might be why it is making funny sounds. What if the bear got hold of it?"

"I am not convinced there is any bear hanging around Brighton. We have just proved that the two bear attacks were faked, so why should we believe there is any such animal around here?"

Clara was about to reply to him on that subject when the bushes parted and something small and brown wandered out. Clara stared at the bundle of fur before her, which was about the size of a medium dog, but far more heavily built and, quite clearly, a bear cub.

"I think we might have solved another mystery," Clara smiled.

The bear cub wandered up to her and patted at her feet with a paw. It was clearly hungry and cold. It nestled into her lap. It was not very old, and Clara picked it up easily in her arms. It didn't seem to mind being held.

"Clara, you are holding a bear," Tommy said to her firmly. "It could bite your face off."

"I don't think it will," Clara replied. "I think it just wants some comfort and some food. Come on, little thing. At least we now know we can call off the hunt."

Ignoring Tommy's protests, Clara headed back up to the house and towards the kitchen. He was a step behind her and heard the sharp shriek from Annie as she spotted the bear.

"I am never going to hear the end of this," Tommy groaned to himself.

The bear cub was ultimately found a new home in a Zoological Gardens where it would be looked after and made sure that it never was hungry again. It proved a sweet little thing, but once it had been fed and had slept, it started to get quite boisterous and had begun to knock about furniture and chew on the table legs. Daisy had been quite glad to find it a more appropriate home. The capture of the bear cub had put a dent in the pride of most of the hunters who had come thinking they were seeking something enormous and, well, full grown. A lot of them who had claimed to have seen the bear now departed as fast as they possibly could, their claims obviously fraudulent. No one, naturally, claimed the reward money. Clara was quite entitled to it; however, she was not interested in claiming it.

Daisy and Edward shut down the Sun Club for the time being. It was not clear if they would open it again in the summer. For the moment, they needed all the guests out of the way and for the police investigation to conclude. The rumours that were going around town were not helping the situation, though at least they had not as yet quite touched upon the truth of the matter. Mrs Gordon's powerful and influential family were making sure that things were kept as quiet as possible, and that the newspapers were being heavily censored on the subject.

There was hope that the truth behind the murders may never come out at all and that at least some of the Sun Club's reputation could be salvaged.

A fortnight after Mrs Gordon had been arrested and charged with the murder of her husband and Mr O'Brien, Clara and Tommy paid a visit to Daisy and Edward. The closed Sun Club seemed a lonely place, the hallways somehow stark without the presence of the guests. Daisy offered them tea in the sitting room.

"Mrs Gordon has confessed," Daisy said when the formalities were over. "The Inspector was good enough to update me. She had been suspicious about her husband for some time and was concerned about his friendship with O'Brien who they had met through the naturist movement. When Mr Gordon suggested the holiday here, he implied to his wife it was an opportunity for them to make amends. Then they arrived and she spied O'Brien.

"She argued with her husband who swore it was all just a coincidence. She almost believed him, until she learned O'Brien had come here alone. That fateful afternoon, she slipped away from the others and confronted O'Brien when she found him alone walking along the cliff edge. According to her, she never meant to push him, and it was all an accident."

"Then how did he end up with claw marks on him?" Clara raised a knowing eyebrow.

"Exactly, Clara. She realised what she had done and then this remarkable idea sprung to her mind. She had been reading that morning about a bear being on the loose and that people should be careful when out alone. Inventing the claw marks would make it seem as if the bear had attacked O'Brien and knocked him down. She hastened back to the house, stole a knife from the kitchen, and made the marks before returning the knife and heading back to the sea to join the others."

"It was fortuitous she did not stumble across us," Clara observed.

"She must have been just ahead of us, I suppose. Anyway, initially everything seemed to work out as she had hoped. Her husband believed his companion had suffered a dreadful accident. Then you started looking into things and Mr Gordon must have overheard us or the police mention that there might not have been a bear. That O'Brien fell over the cliff and that was what killed him. He started to recall how his wife had vanished for such a long time the day of the accident and how she seemed very animated when she returned. He confronted her with his suspicions and said he would tell the police. I do not suppose he thought she would kill him."

"She had to protect herself," Clara saw how things had played out. "She had masked one murder with a bear attack, why not another?"

"It made things even easier for her when one of the other guests said they had seen a bear in the woods," Edward added.

"I hate to say it, but if Drake had not spotted her leaving the house in a raincoat and then returning without it, we would never have looked for it when we did. She could have removed it and destroyed it before the police began their search in the morning. Then we would have had no real evidence against her," Clara remarked.

Daisy did not care to hear that her despised former fiancé had been instrumental in solving the crime. She hastened to change the subject.

"I have spoken discreetly with my solicitor, and he believes the family are pushing forward a case for insanity. I believe the line they are going to follow is that Mrs Gordon was delusional and thought her husband was having an affair with another man, when in fact it was all in her head."

"An interesting conclusion, and one they will likely get away with. The letter is too vague to prove there was a forbidden romance going on and a photograph of three men together is hardly evidence, except that there was a link between Mr Gordon and Mr O'Brien before they arrived here." Clara concurred.

"Exactly, it might save the Sun Club if we can at least avoid talk of risqué love affairs happening behind our doors between men," Daisy nodded.

"We still have the issue that Mrs Gordon's lunacy claim might be linked to naturism," Edward added. "However, the family will presumably need to demonstrate she was showing signs of her illness before she arrived here and that will limit the damage, I suppose."

"We can only do our best to weather this storm," Daisy reached out and clutched Edward's hand. "Whatever happens, we will survive."

They looked more united than ever before, the difficulties they had faced drawing them closer together rather than pulling them apart. Clara was glad for that.

"What of Mr Drake?" She asked.

"He is being charged with trespass and common assault," Edward replied. "He probably will receive some sort of fine, but we have the assurances of our solicitor he will do everything he can to make it clear to Mr Drake he is not to come near Daisy again. Inspector Park-Coombs was very sympathetic and has promised that if Drake is ever seen around the property then we can immediately call the police station and a constable will be dispatched."

"Inspector Park-Coombs is a very good policeman," Clara meant every word. "What about your mother, Edward?"

"She is going to come over for tea on Sunday," Daisy answered promptly. "I have no doubt it will be an interesting evening, but I shall do my best to overcome her."

"I think she will adjust," Edward added. "My mother speaks fiercely, but she is soft as butter really, and, whatever happens, I will not allow us to lose touch as we did once before. Even if she cannot give the Sun Club her blessing, we shall still do everything we can to welcome her here."

Clara thought those were generous words, spoken in the glow of new love when all obstacles seem surmountable. She wondered how long such determination would last once the reality of the situation set in. However, that was not her problem.

"I want to thank you again, Clara, Tommy, for all you did for us. We could not have survived this without your help."

"It was what you hired us to do," Clara smiled. "And we aim to please."

After they had consumed several cups of tea at the Sun Club, Clara and Tommy headed for home.

"I wonder what Reverand Lane makes of all this?" Tommy remarked as they walked.

"I imagine he is beside himself and hopeful the Sun Club is finished."

"Do you think it can survive this?"

Clara shrugged her shoulders.

"I cannot say. Only time will tell. I hope so, however."

Tommy glanced at his sister in some surprise.

"Really, Clara?"

"Really," Clara replied. "It may not be my cup of tea, but I have no reason to wish the naturists harm."

They walked along in thoughtful silence for a few minutes, then Tommy turned to his sister with a big grin on his face.

"So, you and O'Harris fancy having your honeymoon at the Sun Club?"

Clara cast him a look.

"I am sure Daisy would let you stay for free," Tommy teased.

"Be careful," Clara answered back, "or I might just tell Annie I am sending you back to do guard duty on the place when it opens again next summer."

"You wouldn't."

"I would."

Tommy shuddered at the thought.

"Let us just agree to never speak of the Sun Club again."

"Agreed."

Enjoyed this Book?

You can make a difference

As an independent writer reviews of my books are hugely important to help my work reach a wider audience. If you haven't already, I would love it if you could take five minutes to review this book on Amazon.

Thank you very much!

The Clara Fitzgerald Series

Have you read them all?

Memories of the Dead

The first mystery

Flight of Fancy

The second mystery

Murder in Mink

The third mystery

Carnival of Criminals

The fourth mystery

Mistletoe and Murder

The fifth mystery

The Poison Pen

The sixth mystery

Grave Suspicions of Murder

The seventh mystery

The Woman Died Thrice

The eighth mystery

Murder and Mascara

The ninth mystery

The Green Jade Dragon

The tenth mystery

The Monster at the Window

The eleventh mystery

Murder on the Mary Jane

The twelfth mystery

The Missing Wife

The thirteenth mystery

The Traitor's Bones

The fourteenth mystery

The Fossil Murder

The fifteenth mystery

Mr Lynch's Prophecy

The sixteenth mystery

Death at the Pantomime

The seventeenth mystery

The Cowboy's Crime

The eighteenth mystery

The Trouble with Tortoises

The nineteenth mystery

The Valentine Murder

The twentieth mystery

A Body Out of Time

The twenty-first mystery

The Dog Show Affair

The twenty-second mystery

The Unlucky Wedding Guest

The twenty-third mystery

Worse Things Happen at Sea

The twenty-fourth mystery

A Diet of Death

The twenty-fifth mystery

Brilliant Chang Returns

The twenty-sixth mystery

Storm in a Teacup

The twenty-seventh mystery

The Dog Theft Mystery

The twenty-eighth mystery

The Day the Zeppelin Came

The twenty-ninth mystery

The Mystery of Mallory

The thirtieth mystery

Also by Evelyn James

The Gentleman Detective Series

The Gentleman Detective

Norwich 1898.

Colonel Bainbridge, private detective, is wondering if it is time to
hang up his magnifying glass when the arrival of his niece and the
unexpected death of a pugilist has him trying to prove a man innocent
of murder.

Delving into the murky world of street fighting and match fixing, can
they determined who really killed the boxer Simon One-Foot or will
a man who has done no wrong end up swinging for a crime he could
not have committed?

Available on Amazon

About the Author

Evelyn James (aka Sophie Jackson) began her writing career in 2003 working in traditional publishing before embracing the world of ebooks and self-publishing. She has written over 80 books, available on a variety of platforms, both fiction and non-fiction.

You can find out more about Sophie's various titles at her website **www.sophie-jackson.com** or connect through social media on Facebook **www.facebook.com/SophieJacksonAuthor** and if you fancy sending an email do so at **sophiejackson.author@gmail.com**